## THE SURVIVALIST
## THE ORDEAL

John Rourke took his gunship into a dive as the first of the two enemy ships exploded, a fireball washing across the air above him.

Snow and ice pelted against his windshield, the windshield wipers working furiously now.

Mini-guns blazed toward him, Rourke activating a rearward-firing missile as he skimmed over the treetops.

His mouth was bleeding from the fistfight.

A missile contrail skimmed beneath him and he climbed, realized it was a mistake, started the dive as the second contrail arced over his nose.

The corners of John Rourke's mouth turned up. He was tired, hungry for real food—and frightened more than he ever had been in his life because of Natalia.

"Eat it," Rourke almost whispered.

The terrain followed, then rotated one hundred eighty degrees and started to climb. The remaining Soviet gunship was coming for him, dead on, mini-guns firing. A missile contrail.

John Rourke's finger rested over the last of his aft-firing portside missiles.

He let the machine turn one hundred eighty degrees, tail rotor facing the enemy, and touched fire control, the gunship vibrating, Rourke starting the machine into a dive as he looked back.

**The Survivalist series by Jerry Ahern
published by New English Library:**

# The Survivalist 17
# The Ordeal

# Jerry Ahern

**NEW ENGLISH LIBRARY**
Hodder and Stoughton

**British Library Cataloguing C.I.P.**

Ahern, Jerry
 The ordeal.
 I. Title
 813'.54 [F]

ISBN 0 450 50936 2

Printed and bound in Great Britain for Hodder and Stoughton Paperbacks, a division of Hodder and Stoughton Ltd., Mill Road, Dunton Green, Sevenoaks, Kent TN13 2YA. (Editorial Office: 47 Bedford Square, London WC1B 3DP) by Cox & Wyman Ltd., Reading, Berks.

*For our good friends the Gottlebers, Tim, Patti and their son "Little Richard," a future "survivalist" if ever there was one—all the best . . .*

# Chapter One

The vanguard of the black insect shapes of the Soviet gunships was visible for the briefest instant through the front windshield of the van-like German transport. And then they were suddenly there in such great numbers that, as they passed overhead, the fleet of Soviet gunships blocked the sun and darkened the morning. Despite herself, Sarah Rourke screamed and looked behind them. The darkness surrounded them. The German ordinary soldier who drove her hissed something about God in Heaven as gunfire raked the road surface around them on all sides. The Christian Chinese woman sitting toward the rear of the van (she was an interpreter) murmured the name "Jesus." The Chinese functionary beside the woman—a man of about fifty and very staid in appearance and demeanor prior to this, Sarah Rourke had thought—made the sign of the cross.

The van swerved wildly.

Sarah Rourke's hands involuntarily clutched at her abdomen and the child she had carried there for almost four months. The sounds of the electric mini-guns firing from overhead were as she imagined the screams of banshees to have sounded when, as a litle girl, her grandfather had so frighteningly told her the dark tales of Irish folklore and, afterwards at night, she'd been too frightened even to put her hands out from beneath the covers over her bed, too frightened to get up and go to the bathroom. She'd outgrown such fears, and knew she would never outgrow the fear she experienced now.

"Frau Rourke. Hold on, please!"

Sarah Rourke was thrown toward the passenger-side door, but without thinking her hands moved toward the armrest at the center console and she held on. Her eyes moved to the young German's face. His eyes were pinpoints of terror, his cheeks pale and sweat glistening despite the cool temperature inside the vehicle.

She looked forward again. The Soviet gunfire had hit the van just ahead of them; the van rolled over on its right side, flames leaping upward into the morning sunlight from the under-carriage near where, she imagined, the synth fuel tank was. The van had been there to provide security for them. Now—

In the next instant, her own driver shouting something she couldn't comprehend, the driver of the lead van toppled from his overturned vehicle, clambered across it toward the rear of the van, then was blown skyward, his body covered in flames.

She felt as if she would vomit.

A blast of orange flame and black smoke, putrid-smelling even through the climate-control system of the van, washed over the front of the van in which she rode, the German soldier swerving so hard to the left and away from it that she almost fell against his right arm and the steering wheel. The female Chinese interpreter screamed.

The sunlight returned.

As the wheel recovered, Sarah peered through her window, much of it smudged over with smoke and burned synth fuel residue. But she was still able to see. The Soviet gunships weren't turning back. They had nearly disappeared over the horizon, in the direction of the First Chinese City which she had just left.

"I must stop the vehicle, Frau Rourke—the others—"

"Yes! Yes!" The van skidded, fishtailed a little and stopped.

10

"Stay inside, please, Frau Rourke—"

"No—don't be silly!"

The driver's-side door swung outward and he was gone, the fire extinguisher unit from the center console gone, too. Sarah Rourke worked the door open on her side, half stumbling to the ground, the shawl falling from her shoulders, her right hand reaching into the purse she'd had made to carry her pistol. For weeks now, she'd been unable to get into her jeans, let alone a gunbelt. Pants for women were all but unknown among the Icelanders with whom she had lately lived and the pajama-like pants worn by some of the Chinese women here only made her look more pregnant. She had gone back to the high-waisted ankle-length skirts and frilly blouses of the Icelanders as the only thing she could wear. Her left hand bunched her skirt up as she ran now, the Trapper Scorpion .45 cocked and safety off in her right hand, but useless, she knew, against the Soviet gunships should they return.

Her driver was spraying the cab of the overturned van, but it was pointless, she realized; the flames were out of control.

The woman interpreter and the functionary were flanking her.

The third van of the convoy pulled over by the side of the road, Chinese soldiers, even the Chinese chairman, bolting from the vehicle, one of the men with a fire extinguisher, another of them with a heavy blanket.

If Colonel Mann's fleet of J-7Vs would only come . . .

Bjorn Rolvaag opened his eyes when he heard the first sounds. They were very much muted, he thought. But they still sounded like the gunfire with which he had become so familiar since the five centuries of global warfare had come to Lydveldid Island. His head ached and he remembered now. He had been injured—shot in the head?

He remembered the voice of Doctor Rourke, the father of Annie. And, despite the pain in his head, Rolvaag smiled at the thought of her. She had spoken to him while he had been—unconscious? But somehow, he knew she had been thinking of him and that she had said something about Hrothgar; Rolvaag somehow knew too that the animal was cared for.

Why was there gunfire here in the peaceful Chinese city?

Bjorn Rolvaag let his eyes drift over his body. A tube was attached to him by a vein in his left arm. He followed the tube. It was an I.V. from a bottle of clear liquid he deduced likely was something like glucose. Before he had chosen the lonely life of a policeman, he had studied many things in the fine schools of his homeland.

His right arm felt stiff but seemed to work and his fingers, though they felt thick, flexed. Bjorn Rolvaag tore the I.V. from his arm. It hurt for a split second, but as he moved his left arm there was only a lingering soreness.

Rolvaag touched his hands gingerly to his head and face. His beard was as it should be, but he felt bandages over the top of his head. Had they shaved away his hair to operate on him? He mentally shrugged, as it would probably grow back.

There was a closet in the corner of the room and he surmised that if his clothing were anywhere, it would be there.

He was hearing the sounds of gunfire louder than before.

The instant he attempted to sit up in bed, the floor beneath him shook and he fell back, hearing the sound of an explosion and then another and another.

It was not time for a man to rest in bed like a sick child.

He sat up and the pain he felt in his head was unlike anything he had ever known. His fists balled closed. His teeth gritted together. Rolvaag fought his body to control his breathing and the pain eased slightly, enough at least that he could open his eyes. Floaters moved across them and he squeezed his eyes tight shut, then opened them again. That only made them worse.

He would live with the floaters until they passed. He moved his legs from beneath the sheet and blanket and slung them over the side of the bed.

This caused the floaters to increase and a terrible dizziness began in him.

More gunfire, another explosion, the floor trembling again, but less violently than the first time.

Rolvaag eyed the closet. If his clothes were there, all well and good. But if his staff were there . . .


Machine-gun fire stitched down on both sides of him, but there was nothing else for it but to keep going and reach the chopper.

Akiro Kurinami ran faster now than he could ever remember running in his life, across the snow-splotched tarmac, snow falling in large white flakes, the kind of flakes he had first seen as a boy when he had been taken to visit relatives in Sapporo. On all sides of him, German gunships were going airborne, and overhead the Soviet gunships were making their strafing runs.

His ears rang with the cacophony of the warfare surrounding him, but he kept moving.

A German gunship fifty yards to his left was struck— perhaps the mini-guns or perhaps an air-to-ground missile. There was an earsplittingly loud crack. The ground under him trembled and he was pitched into the snow. A black, yellow and orange fireball was belching skyward, the swirl of white surrounding it making it almost surreal-seeming, like something out of a nightmare.

Kurinami was on his knees. German gunships were rising on all sides of him, some beginning to engage the enemy before they had even reached a safe altitude. Kurinami got to his feet.

He ran toward the nearest of the just-activating machines,

its number the one to which he had been assigned. German maintenance technicians were trained for just such an occurrence as this—a surprise attack—trained to warm up the helicopters the instant the command to scramble was given so that by the time the pilots reached them, the machines could be instantly airborne.

Kurinami half fell through the half-open fuselage door. "I'm Kurinami! Where's the doorgunner?"

"I do not know, Herr Lieutenant!"

"Then you're my doorgunner. Belt in!" And Kurinami was up into the body of the gunship, moving forward, then sliding down into the cockpit seat.

All systems were up. "Get that fuselage door locked open all the way!"

Through his headset, as he pulled it on, he heard the man saying, "But Herr Lieutenant Kurinami—"

"What is it, soldier?"

"I have only fired this weapon once before—and only for testing, Herr Lieutenant."

"Consider this your big opportunity, then." And Akiro Kurinami reached for the controls of the main rotor. He thought of Elaine Halversen. A smile crossed his lips. And he said into the teardrop-shaped microphone just in front of his mouth, "We're airborne—now!"

The German helicopter gunship slipped left slightly and began to rise, rotating a full three hundred sixty degrees, then angling sharply upward, enemy gunfire coming in along the portside fuselage as Kurinami pulled out more speed. "Don't wait for my command to fire—open up on targets of opportunity."

"Yes, Herr Lieutenant!"

"Then do it now!" The drafted doorgunner opened fire. It would be hard to miss, Kurinami thought, zig-zagging his way up to a better fighting altitude. There were enemy gunships on all sides of them.

14

Just over the horizon line, barely visible in the snowfall, fireballs were rising from Eden Base; the black Soviet gunships circled around it like a ring, missile contrails streaking from sky to ground.

Kurinami changed pitch and banked to starboard, under three of the enemy gunships closest to him, rotating one hundred eighty degrees, activating his starboardside missile pod. He fired as he accelerated away, and two of the enemy gunships exploded, the third visibly exploding as he glanced back once.

Through his chin bubble now, he could see more of the German gunships rising from the base field just outside Eden, their mini-guns blazing tongues of flame toward the Soviet attackers.

But still, there was Eden Base.

Kurinami increased speed, almost redlining. He could hear the doorgunner as he engaged with Soviet gunships trailing them. Kurinami activated one of the aft-firing air-to-air/air-to-ground missiles from his portside pod, his targeting on manual where he liked it, the green electronic outline of the Russian gunship floating under his bullseye and away, then starting under again. Kurinami touched the fire control.

"We got him, Herr Lieutenant!"

"Keep shooting somebody else, then!"

Ahead, the topography surrounding Eden Base took greater shape, greater definition. And so did the ring of death surrounding it . . .

Bjorn Rolvaag threw modesty to the winds. Clad in nothing but his hospital gown, the massive staff old Jon the swordmaker had crafted for him in his hands, he threw open the door to his hospital room and stepped into the corridor.

White-clad Chinese nurses were wheeling patients from their rooms, some in chairs, others on gurneys. There was

15

smoke billowing along the corridor in the direction from which they came.

Rolvaag's fists bunched on his staff.

A nurse ran up to him, said something totally unintelligible, screamed as another explosion came, then tried dragging him off by the left arm. He let her tug at his arm for a moment. She pounded her tiny fists on his chest, shrieking at him.

Rolvaag smiled down at her.

She ran off.

Rolvaag stared along the length of the corridor.

There was no need wearing down his meager energy reserves in going to meet this enemy, whoever it was, because it was apparent the enemy was coming rapidly enough to meet him.

Rolvaag leaned heavily against the corridor wall. Communist Russians, perhaps? Probably.

Would his dog be safe?

He was glad the young girl Annie Rourke had married the fine young man Mr. Rubenstein. They looked well together, the way people did when they were in love truly.

Through the smoke, he saw movement.

Men in black—and they were not Chinese—were running along the corridor.

Bjorn Rolvaag pushed himself away from the corridor wall and held his staff before him diagonally, bisecting his body left shoulder to right hip.

In his own language, the only language he had ever known and ever seen any purpose in knowing, he shouted, "Halt where you are! This is a place for sick people to become well, not a place for the likes of you!" The Icelandic tongue was rich in literature, was beautifully spoken. The coming of the Rourkes, the coming of the Germans, the warfare with the Russians, the hospitality of the Chinese in their flower-shaped First City—nothing compelled him to learn a tongue different from his own.

The Russian woman—she was very sweet and very sad and,

perhaps even more because of that, so very beautiful—the
Russian woman, Major Tiemerovna, could converse with him
and he with her, although it was awkward. But it was adequate.

It would have been nice to speak with Annie Rourke
Rubenstein, though.

Bjorn Rolvaag dismissed such thoughts from his mind.

The black-uniformed men—Soviet KGB Elite Corps commandoes—were approaching slowly, their rifles and pistols
drawn, perplexed looks in their eyes and faces. Should they
shoot this man? He smiled at such thoughts. But of course they
should. Because once a few of them came within range of his
staff, he would begin soundly cracking their skulls.

The Russians spoke to him. He understood enough of that,
although it didn't sound pretty as it did when Major
Tiemerovna spoke to him. But he understood enough of that to
know that they meant to kill him. There again lay the
superfluity of language.

He had known that much just looking into their faces.

Bjorn Rolvaag moved into the center of the corridor, his
staff still in his hands.

A soldier who looked barely teen-aged lunged at him with the
naked muzzle of a rifle and Rolvaag dodged him easily,
although the sudden motion made his head ache and caused
the floaters to return. He had hardly realized before that they
were gone.

The boy soldier lunged again and Rolvaag took a half step
left and moved the staff twice, but fewer than ten degrees
outward, the base of the staff impacting this bothersome little
enemy in the groin once and once on the tip of the jaw. The
Russian felt flat on his back in the middle of the corridor.

A soldier raised his rifle to his shoulder.

Rolvaag started to confront him.

From behind him, he heard more of the impossible to
fathom Chinese words.

But he thought it might be wise to take cover. In one fluid

motion, his staff swept outward and brought the rifleman down at the heels. Rolvaag flattened his own body on the corridor floor, his head swimming with pain, his right hand holding his staff, his left hand clutched around the neck of the Russian whom he was choking to death. Gunfire rang through the corridor all around him, but most heavily from behind him.

Guns were so terribly noisy.

Booted feet ran past him, the clanging of military equipment, the gunfire again.

He looked at the second Russian's face. It was purple enough and he let go.

There were blood-stained white trousers in front of him, now, and Rolvaag looked up along their length and then up the body contour—a female body contour—and into the prettiest Chinese face he had seen here.

She smiled at him as she dropped to her knees beside him.

She told him something he didn't understand.

He told her she was very pretty, knowing she would understand him no more than he had understood her.

She was trying to help him stand up.

And so he did that, but his head hurt very badly; not, he confessed to himself, so badly that he needed to hold on to her quite so tightly as he did when she helped him back into his room. But almost . . .


They had all moved into one van, presenting less of a target on the road leading to the site of the soon-to-be-begun German outpost, lest the Soviet gunships should return.

But Sarah Rourke doubted that they would—not until they were through destroying the First Chinese City.

In the distance, the high plateau rose ahead of them, stretching for miles, it seemed. But she knew the area to the last foot, having tramped across it at the request of Colonel Mann and worked with one of his engineering officers and a

18

staff of men to do rough sketchwork preparatory to an overall plan for the base. At first, she had thought Mann's corresponding with her personally by military messenger might have been something put together by her husband, John Rourke, and the commander of the Forces of New Germany in Argentina, just to keep her busy. But it hadn't proven out that way. It had seemed logical to Mann that with a professional artist available on the scene—albeit her professional experience was from five centuries before and in the rather left-handed field of children's literature—the preliminary sketchwork could be handled with adequate efficiency. She had never so labored over drawings since the acceptance of her first published illustrations.

The van was moving inexorably nearer to the plateau, the hermetically sealed German tents seeming barren, lonely there, the few men of the temporary garrison in full battle gear, their solitary anti-aircraft emplacement sandbagged and manned, men with assault rifles at the entrance that would pass them through the electrified perimeter.

The tents were so few as to be missable from high-altitude observation unless one were specifically looking for them, and extrapolating the flight path of the Soviet gunships, they would have passed out of visual range of the base. Hence, the few men here were still alive and there was still hope that Colonel Mann and his J-7Vs could do something.

The chairman of the First Chinese City spoke to her for the first time since they had entered the van. "I am hopeful, Mrs. Rourke, that there is some chance. My city will be in ruins within the hour if the aerial attack is not, somehow, forced to cease."

The security waved them through and the van continued on until it stopped before the largest of the few tents arranged with geometric precision here on the plateau.

To have returned to the First City, despite the fact that it would have taken considerably longer to get there, would have been pointless. The Chinese here had a substantial and well-equipped army, but nothing to combat airpower except will and courage.

The chairman rose and began to alight from the van, Sarah gathering her skirt and following after him. He helped her down.

A young German officer—a lieutenant—came to attention, saluting them, offering his hand to the chairman who received it, bowing as he offered his hand to her. He held her hand briefly as if it were something very fragile. He'd evidently never seen her fire a gun, wrangle a horse, butcher a chicken or change a diaper.

A stiff, cold wind was blowing over the plateau; the two German gunships that serviced the tent base vibrated on their moorings. She cocooned the heavy Icelandic shawl tighter about her, grateful for the length which brought it nearly to her knees.

"I have been in radio contact with my colonel, Herr Chairman, Frau Rourke."

"And?" She couldn't help herself; the word spilled out of her.

The German officer—he was young, blond, blue-eyed, perfect-looking—made a great show of shooting the cuff of his uniform blouse and looking at his wristwatch. "In precisely five minutes and forty-three seconds, the Herr Colonel's personal aircraft will touch down. The Herr Colonel has requested, Frau Rourke, that one from among this party join him aboard the J-7V to facilitate targeting recognition factors once the squadron has reached the site of the First City prior to engaging the enemy."

She wanted to kiss him. Instead, she said, "I'll go."

The chairman of the First Chinese City merely sighed.

If there were anything to pre-natal predestination, what would the child she carried inside her become, Sarah Rourke suddenly wondered. She smiled at the thought. Because she

20

already knew. Like her son, like her daughter, this child, male or female, would be a Rourke. "Is there someplace where I can go to the bathroom before Colonel Mann lands? Pregnancy does that to you."

The young German officer looked taken aback.

Sarah Rourke shrugged her shoulders and smiled.

# Chapter Two

"Your hands are crushing me," Annie whispered up at him softly, gently.

Paul Rubenstein realized that they were. But he held his wife anyway, slightly easing the grip his hands had on her shoulders. She was kneeling beside her brother, treating the headwound Michael had sustained at the hands of the forces of the Second Chinese City. An errant gust of wind played with her long hair. In the distance, beyond the confines of the black-hued, bare rock cave's overhang, the sounds of battle raged on. A few feet beyond Michael lay the Russian officer, passed into something more like sleep than unconsciousness. When they had reached the cave, the Russian had murmured in well-spoken but heavily accented English, "Why did he try to save me?"

Paul Rubenstein had had no answer for the man.

Black smoke filled the sky to the north and west. All of it reminded him of the prophecies of Armageddon in the Christian New Testament.

They had hidden the Specials, their New Germany-crafted high-tech weapons-equipped motorcycles, deeper within the cave. But much of what was needed for the weapons pods to be functional had been expended during the raid against the Second Chinese City which had resulted in Michael's and the injured Russian officer's rescue. There was an adequate supply of synth fuel, but there was nowhere to go. Enemy forces seemed to surround them totally.

Otto Hammerschmidt and Han Lu Chen stood guard in the rocks above the overhang; Maria Leuden stood with her hands in front of her, one resting in the other, a look of total helplessness on her ashen face. Paul wondered absently whether she wished her doctorate were in medicine now rather than archeology.

Paul Rubenstein looked back at his wife when she spoke. "It looks like superficial bleeding. But we don't have any way of telling whether or not it's anything more. Daddy always told me that you treat what you can find and try to treat what you can't. I wish he were here," Annie whispered.

Paul Rubenstein took this as no reflection on his own talents or abilities, such as they were or weren't. That John Rourke, Michael's and Annie's father, his best friend, would be an asset under any circumstances was a foregone conclusion. Two men in need of medical treatment only underlined the imperative.

But John Thomas Rourke, Doctor of Medicine, survival and weapons expert, the very embodiment of the phrase "Socratic man," wasn't here.

After they had begun to effect the rescue of Michael and, coincidentally, saved the Russian officer as well, Natalia had been injured somehow and John Rourke had delegated her Special to Han Lu Chen, taking Natalia aboard his own. They had been forced to escape via a different route. And nothing had been seen of them since. Natalia had been hospitalized prior to going on the rescue mission, declared herself well, seemed her old self—or had she? Paul Rubenstein wondered.

The radios in their helmets worked perfectly and, logic dictated, so did those in the identical helmets worn by John and Natalia when they were last seen. Yet John and Natalia couldn't be raised, meaning something was very wrong or they were out of range.

Already, Paul Rubenstein planned to combat the second possibility.

But what disturbed him—more even than their current

plight in the middle of what seemed like full-blown warfare between Soviet Air Cavalry and the hard-line Communist surface armies of the Second Chinese City—were the remarks of Han Lu Chen concerning Natalia. That she had seemed totally unaware of what was happening, could only murmur John's name, that something seemed so terribly wrong about her.

And as all of them had fled into the mountains to escape the battle, Annie had said to him through her helmet radio, "I can feel something—it's Natalia, Paul."

Paul Rubenstein dropped to his knees beside his wife. Her hands had begun gently to dress Michael's headwound. "What did you mean about Natalia?"

"Before?"

"Is there something now?"

"She's very sick. I can feel her thoughts inside of me and they're meaningless. The only thing I do . . . understand . . . the only thing I do feel strongly enough to understand besides that is sadness, that she's so filled with sadness. It's like she's inside some deep pit and she can't quite see the top, knowing that there's something still outside beyond it. She's afraid."

He stared into his wife's eyes. She wasn't looking at him, wasn't looking at anything.

It was a different sort of vision.

And, though she'd always had it since adulthood, perhaps before, a chill ran along his spine. Such an ability—or curse—frightened him. And he knew it frightened Annie. "Where is she, Annie?"

Annie's eyes didn't flicker, although she blinked. "Cold. Very cold. I can feel Daddy's thoughts near to her, but it's like a bad radio transmission. I can just tell that he's there. What's in her is so strong, it's like—" And Annie bent her head forward, her face going down into her hands as she began to weep.

The voice made him jump slightly and he began reaching for the battered Browning High Power in the tanker holster

24

beneath the open front of his arctic parka.

"This woman—your wife—she sees through the mind?"

Paul folded Annie against him, turned and looked at the Russian officer. The man was sitting up, his head lolled forward, both hands to it as though he were in pain or very tired, what Paul could see of the face nearly as pale as death.

"Yes. She does," Paul Rubenstein answered.

"Can she see the future, too, then?"

"I don't think so."

"I have no such abilities, sir. But for us, here, no special talents are needed. We are all dead. We breathe and move about and hope. But, in the end, we are all dead certainly."

Paul Rubenstein didn't say anything to him after that.

He just held Annie close to him.

The Russian was, most probably, correct.

# Chapter Three

Natalia's eyes, the incredible blueness of them—but they only stared emptily, as though looking through him, not seeing him.

John Rourke held Natalia's nearly naked body close against him and had for some time, but still she trembled. It was not the hypothermia his physician's instincts had first feared, the result of the Special crashing over the edge of the precipice into the icy, raging waters from which he had pulled her. It was something inside her that made her shake, something inside her that was keeping the warmth from his body from warming her.

It was something far worse.

He had been trained as a physician, not a psychiatrist. But piecing it all together over the past weeks, over the past days, now— It was suddenly, piteously, abundantly clear.

For a physician without the proper cross-training in psychoanalysis to indulge in speculative diagnosis based on manifested symptoms of mental disorder was just as likely to be amazingly accurate as asking a television repairman—but there were no such persons, he imagined, these days—to diagnose the origin of persistent abdominal pain.

But here, in the middle of a war, cut off from everyone but each other, he was the only game in town.

Natalia Anastasia Tiemerovna, Major, Committee for State

26

Security of the Soviet, Retired, was perhaps as seriously mentally ill as one could become. She had lost all touch with reality. She was in the depths of a depressive phase he wished he did not interpret as classic manic-depression.

The affair at the Soviet underwater city, where she had faced imminent death at the hands of her psychotic husband, had been brutalized, the victim of heavy-handed drug-induced interrogation sessions, threatened with torture, witnessed his—John Rourke's—own apparent death, been rescued, learned of his—Rourke's—survival, then intentionally placed her own life in jeopardy all over again for the good of others. The fight between him and Vladimir Karamatsov. Both of them—he and Karamatsov—at the point of death. And then, using a knife, wielding it with both her tiny hands like some sort of medieval broadsword, she had cleaved her husband's head from his body.

He remembered her face, then.

And then the assassination attempts in the First Chinese City. Nearly killed again. But before that, after that, the depression, the tears she had unsuccessfully attempted to keep hidden.

And the summoning of will, in what he realized now was a manic state, when she had forced herself along with them on the mission to save Michael, but the depressive stage tugging at her throughout it all. And, finally, the violence, Michael nearly killed, nearly torn limb from limb at the hands of madmen.

Unlike the rest of them—himself, his wife, his son and daughter, his daughter's husband Paul, all survivors from five centuries ago and the days before and after the Night of the War—she had no one.

And he, himself, Rourke realized, had done that to her.

Natalia loved him. He loved Natalia. He loved his wife, Sarah. And Sarah carried his child.

Honor.

27

Cold.

Collapse.

His arms bound more tightly around her, one of the twin Detonics .45s in his right hand. She kept repeating his name, over and over, lifelessly.

John Rourke wept.

# Chapter Four

Colonel Mann's hands on the control yoke of the J-7V reminded her of a lover's hands, caressing something of which he was very fond, very possessive.

She could hear his voice through the headset he had provided her. She sat beside him in the co-pilot's seat in the J-7V's cockpit. "This is Iron Cross Leader. Red Leader, do you copy? Over."

The voice of the right wing commander came in with surprising clarity, but Sarah Rourke realized that her knowledge of radio was several centuries behind the times. Perhaps it wasn't even radio, but some sort of microwave transmission. "This is Red Leader, Herr Colonel. I am reading you. Over."

"This is Iron Cross Leader. Red Leader, you are to execute. I repeat—execute. Do you copy? Over."

"This is Red Leader. Affirmative. Execute, Iron Cross Leader. Red Leader out."

"Iron Cross Leader out." In an instant, the right wing commander's element broke off in a steep bank toward the north. Colonel Mann's voice began again. "This is Iron Cross Leader. Black Leader, I say execute. Do you copy? Over."

The voice of the left wing commander, younger sounding, higher pitched, almost feminine in a way, came back. "This is Black Leader, Colonel. I copy execute. Black Leader out."

"Iron Cross Leader out." The left wing element banked right

and down, passing beneath them, going toward the north as well. Ahead, a ring of black Soviet helicopter gunships encircled the exposed petals of the flower-shaped First Chinese City. Fires were everywhere and ant-sized figures darted along the ground. An explosion belched upward toward them. She heard Mann's voice telling her, "Please do not be frightened, Frau Rourke. This aircraft can both outmaneuver and outspeed the Soviet gunships and, thanks to recent innovations of our engineers, outgun their aircraft as well. Rest easily. Please alert me to any particularly sensitive areas where our fire might precipitate greater damage that we might prevent, if you will."

"Certainly, Colonel Mann."

"Thank you, Frau Rourke." Another explosion that seemed just off the tip of the right wing—starboard, she mentally corrected. "This is Iron Cross Leader. Iron Cross element, execute. I say again, execute. Keep with me. We're going in." Colonel Mann glanced to his left, then with an element of sternness in his voice she was unused to, said, "Hoffsteder—tighten up!"

"Yes, Herr Colonel."

"Remenschneider—take the two over the water tower-shaped object."

Sarah Rourke had a slight sensation of motion in the pit of her stomach and, had it been later in her term, she would have blamed the baby. "Colonel—that funnel-shaped area to your left. That's the main entrance into the city. From there, Soviet troops could utilize the monorail system to reach any part of it."

"I understand, Frau Rourke. Thank you." Already the plane was beginning to dive. She realized her nails were gouging into the armrests of her seat. "This is Iron Cross Leader. Jahns—watch my tail. Do you copy? Over."

"This is Iron Cross Three. I copy, Iron Cross Leader. Over."

"Iron Cross Leader out."

Seven Soviet gunships formed an arc several hundred yards

back from the entrance to the tunnel through which access to the First City was gained, mini-guns licking tongues of flame toward barricaded defenders there, missile contrails zig-zagging white plumes of smoke across each other, small explosions belching upward with every-other-second regularity by the entrance itself. Sarah wondered how long the Soviet armada could keep it up without running out of ammunition.

The J-7V barrel-rolled and as she sucked in her breath in what felt as if it would become a scream, Mann's voice reassured her through the headset, "Forgive me, Frau Rourke. An enemy gunship. I shall prevent such an event reoccurring." She watched his fingers move over the weapons console, like the hand of an artist, a toggle switch flipped, a button pushed. There was a slight vibration and she realized he had fired a missile. Her eyes were mesmerized by its contrail, and one of the Soviet gunships in the arc of seven suddenly seemed to stop-frame in mid-air, then vaporized, a black and red fireball expanding outward in all directions. The J-7V banked sharply left—to port, she told herself—and the fireball vanished from her field of vision. His hands moved again. Two of the Soviet gunships rotated a full one hundred eighty degrees, mini-guns blazing.

But her eyes followed the tracer rounds from the J-7V's machine guns, streaks of white and orange against the gray blue of the sky, the farther of the two Soviet gunships suddenly on fire. The J-7V banked sharply to starboard, Mann almost cooing to her, "Forgive me again, Frau Rourke—should this prove—"

"No—I'm fine—the baby, too."

"You are most gracious, Frau Rourke." Another tremor through the aircraft, a contrail, a streak of machine-gun fire, the second Soviet gunship suddenly losing tail control, chunks of the tail rotor flying in all directions, a puff of gray smoke, then a black ball of smoke, orange tongues licking outward hungrily from inside it, then a fireball and the Soviet gunship was gone.

31

The J-7V banked to port and climbed, Sarah Rourke pressed back into her seat, the sensation not at all unpleasant, not like a roller coaster ride, more like a gentle nudge. When Annie and Michael were little, she and John had taken them to a carnival and Michael had eaten so much and John would only go on the little children's rides if any and she had taken them on the roller coaster and been so *sick!* "Colonel!"

"I apologize again, Frau Rourke—alert me should you experience difficulty."

He had begun a power dive. She'd seen William Holden or somebody do this in a movie once and— "Look out!"

"Not to worry, Frau Rourke!" Machine guns from both port and starboard weapons pods were firing; a Soviet gunship exploded less than two hundred yards from them. The J-7V was climbing again. Colonel Mann had warned her, after all, tried to reason with her that she shouldn't be his tactical guide, but it had seemed like a good idea at the *time!* "We are almost out of this, Frau Rourke. Alert me should there be any difficulty, please." She thought it was called a barrel roll. He was into and out of it before she could speak. All she had had time to do was suck in her breath. But now the aircraft vibrated once, then quickly again, two missile contrails arcing away from beneath each wing, two Soviet gunships exploding almost simul-taneously, one on either side of them.

The J-7V banked sharply left and they were flying on their side. She thought she'd be sick. They were into level flight again.

More Soviet gunships were moving toward them like metal filings toward a magnet. "Colonel!"

"I see them, Frau Rourke. This was an excellent area to select. You are to be congratulated."

He banked right—starboard. "Colonel!"

"I see them, Frau Rourke." Two Soviet gunships coming down out of a cloud bank. "Jahns—cover me!"

"Yes, Herr Colonel!"

The J-7V banked to port, went through something that felt

like a half roll, then began to climb. Before she could speak, they were level again. She thought she might throw up! "Colonel—I don't mean to—"

"Yes—he fired a missile. Hold on, Frau Rourke, please!" The J-7V was rolling, an explosion just off their starboard wingtip.

A dive. Her nails—she'd been trying to grow them again—gouged the armrests. They were level again. Tracer patterns to right and left. The chin bubble of one of the Soviet gunships exploded and in the next instant the main rotor spun off and the gunship dropped from sight.

"One more for the moment, Frau Rourke."

One more—one *more!* "Colonel Mann!"

The black shape of the gunship seemed mere feet from the nose of the J-7V and suddenly the J-7V shuddered, there was a split second of contrail and they banked sharply to port. The gunship, visible now through her side window, vaporized in a ball of flames.

The J-7V leveled off. "Jahns—take Iron Cross element and clean up. Iron Cross Leader out."

They were going for altitude. "I should not have so indulged myself, Frau Rourke. We shall observe for now."

"Thank you, Colonel." She looked at her hands—they were white except for under her nails, where they were purple.

# Chapter Five

Akiro Kurinami stepped down from the German helicopter gunship, snow swirling almost lazily beneath the slowly spinning main rotor.

He wiped his bare palms down along the sides of his flight suit. It was cold and the sweat on his hands made him suddenly colder.

Beside him stood the drafted doorgunner. He looked at the young German. "You did well. You can fly with me anytime."

"Thank you, Herr Lieutenant."

Kurinami extended his hand to the man and they shook.

All around them there was devastation. The landing pads were pitted and blackened with shell holes, some seeming deep enough that a man might well have been able to stand in the bottom of one and not have been able to see over the edge. He remembered the tales told of World War One—the War to End All Wars—of how men had sometimes fallen into such shell holes and drowned.

At least a half dozen gunships had never made it off the ground, their structural bones still smoldering in grotesque death postures. At least five more gunships had been shot out of the air.

Had not Colonel Wolfgang Mann more than twenty-four hours earlier more than doubled the size of the force here, victory for the Soviet attackers would have been a certainty. Much of the new construction for Eden Base, as it was, lay in ruins. One of the shuttle craft was heavily damaged and another had sustained what appeared from the air at least to have been only minor damage.

He had no idea of casualties and, deep inside himself, didn't want to know. Despite the friction between himself and Christopher Dodd, Eden commander, there was a kinship with his fellow astronauts, a kinship grown out of having survived the five centuries since the Night of the War, having survived together. Losing one of them was like the loss of a brother or sister.

Kurinami's own wife and family had died during the flaming aftermath of the Night of the War, when the very atmosphere itself had ionized and the sky caught fire and nearly all life on earth vanished. Or before, perhaps, on the Night of the War itself. He would never know. And he desperately wanted the killing to stop. Now and forever.

The Soviet gunships had fallen back; some pockets of fighting were still in the environs of Eden Base where Soviet commandoes had rappeled in from the cargo bays of the gunships, but the back of the attack had been broken. The presence of Soviet land forces, even in such token numbers, augured a major offensive. Would Eden Base be able to withstand it? Would German supplies of ordnance and spare parts and synth fuel be able to support a protracted defense?

He kept walking, past the potholes, toward the command center, the near edge of the forward side fire-blackened but otherwise seeming undamaged.

The new German commandant, Captain Horst Bremen, stood before it, his curly blond hair wind-tousled, his left cheek dark-smudged, his uniform collar open, an assault rifle in his right hand.

"Kurinami! Over here!"

Kurinami quickened his pace; the German officer strode purposefully toward him. They met beside the remains of one of the helicopters, the acrid smell of still-smoldering synth-fuel residue assailing his nostrils as the wind, bitterly cold,

35

suddenly shifted. "You agree they will return?"

"Yes, Captain. It seems inevitable from the pattern of their attack."

"Yes—inevitable. But we must forestall the inevitable. I have instructed that headquarters in New Germany be concerned and emergency reinforcements and supplies be dispatched to us at once. But at the very least, we are looking at eighteen precious hours, perhaps as long as thirty-six hours until reinforcements arrive. New Germany itself has been attacked, but the Soviet force was easily repelled. More a harassing action, it appears. Soviet forces are attacking the First Chinese City, the Herr Colonel personally supervising the counterattack. A significant concentration of ground forces is attacking our base outside the Hekla Community in Lydveldid Island. It seems, however, that this area is critical to the Russians. Therefore, we cannot allow it to be overrun. Another attack like this one might be more than we can sustain. Certainly not a third. I need you to volunteer."

"Volunteer?" Kurinami echoed.

"I believe it advisable to dispatch a small force of gunships and ground troops to the north. If possible, locate the Soviet staging area and counterattack, something logic dictates they will not suspect us capable of. As they advance, fight holding actions designed to delay them as much as possible. If you choose not to volunteer, I will not think any the less of you. But, logic again—I am told you are the best pilot available and you have some significant experience versus our adversaries which my other officers lack. It may prove a mission from which you will not return."

"When was there any other kind of mission?" Akiro Kurinami almost whispered.

"Then you will do it?"

"Will I have time—" Kurinami began.

"Your Fraulein Doctor is helping with the wounded, Lieutenant. The appropriate machines should be ready within

36

the next fifteen minutes." And Bremen glanced at his chronometer.

"The man who was my doorgunner—he's just a technician, but I'd like him along as doorgunner again. He's a good man."

"Consider it done, although I must go through the formality of asking. By its very nature, this is a force of volunteers you will lead."

"I understand," Akiro Kurinami nodded . . .


"I don't understand!" Tears flowed from her pretty eyes as she spoke. Kurinami took Elaine Halversen into his arms, holding her close against him, trying to blot out the moans of the injured just beyond the gray curtain that separated the tiny alcove in the main hangar building's annex from the hastily set up field hospital. "I don't—why do you—"

"Why are you here, helping the wounded? Why aren't you doing something easier?"

"I—damn your logic!" And she buried her head against his chest. "Don't die—please?"

He wanted very much to promise her that he wouldn't. Instead, he only held her and touched his lips to her forehead, rocking her in his arms.

# Chapter Six

Paul Rubenstein braked the Super, Otto Hammerschmidt, beside him, doing the same. Paul spoke into his helmet headset. "John—do you read me? This is Paul. Come in, John. Over."

Paul Rubenstein looked at Otto Hammerschmidt, the German commando captain's face shield pushed up, his light-colored eyes clearly visible, the worry that was etched on Hammerschmidt's face evident there in his eyes as well.

There was no answer to the radio call.

Rubenstein repeated it, then again. And, then, again.

They had left Annie and Michael and Maria and Han Lu Chen and the Russian officer in the overhang of the cave, Michael still not coming around. They had ridden the Supers some fifteen miles closer to the Second Chinese City, dangerously near the battle lines, nearer, Rubenstein hoped, to wherever it was John and Natalia were in hiding, within their radio range.

He tried the signal again, Hammerschmidt monitoring on his own helmet set.

There was no response.

The wind blew cold and there was the smell of synth fuel heavy on the air—the origin of the odor perhaps some modern equivalent of napalm in use by the Russians against the Second City.

"What if they are dead?"

The voice didn't come through his headset radio. And it was Hammerschmidt's voice. Paul Rubenstein removed his own helmet, as Hammerschmidt had done, ran his fingers through his thinning black hair, settled the helmet over his console. "They aren't dead."

"You mean that you refuse to accept the concept that they might be dead."

"I mean they aren't dead. We'll head north, maybe come on some sign of them, maybe get into their radio range."

"Perhaps encounter some Soviet gunships along the way. What about your wife? What about Michael? Let me go on alone. There's no one waiting for me. That's the best way for a soldier, I think."

"Maybe it is. But no. I'm going on. I'd be glad for your company. But I'm going on anyway."

And Otto Hammerschmidt laughed. Paul Rubenstein looked at him quizzically. "We are strange creatures, I think. As men, I mean. You will search until you find John Rourke and if you do find this man who is your best friend, you will shake his hand, and if you embrace him, you will feel self-conscious and then you will laugh and he will laugh. I had a close friend named Fritz when I was a boy. We used to like to climb in the mountains near the Complex although heights were never my favorite thing. But of course I would not admit that. The rope became snagged and in trying to clear it, the rope frayed and with both our weights, snapped. Fritz fell from sight. I clung to the ledge, eventually got myself to safety and tried roping down to Fritz. I could not. I called to him and there was no answer. I began to cry and I sniffed back the tears and I ran for help. I found a patrol on some sort of compass course, brought them to the scene and they roped down for Fritz. He was unconscious. He revived in the hospital and eventually was fully restored. Fritz was like my brother then. And when I went to visit him in the hospital, we shook hands very briefly. I told him a dirty joke I had heard, something about a Jew, oddly enough." And Hammerschmidt looked at Rubenstein embarrassedly. "But we were taught to think that way and only some of us learned otherwise in those days. But I never told Fritz how frightened I was that he had died, that we might never climb together again, or share secrets with one another. I never even told my father that I cried when I thought Fritz might be dead. No wonder women think we are crazy. They are right. We are." Otto Hammerschmidt pulled his helmet on over his close-cropped blond hair.

Paul Rubenstein put his helmet on as well. "John—do you read me? This is Paul. Over." There was no answer . . .


The shivering was stopped and once he was certain of it, he wrapped Natalia in everything warm there was available to them. Clad only in his still damp light blue cotton shirt and his underpants, John Rourke crouched in the rocks beside her, the small fire between them, his hands busy at disassembling the radio set in his helmet. His jeans and his bootsocks, along with her clothing and her underwear, were drying beside the fire. He had risked it because the need for dry clothing outweighed the potential hazards of such a small fire being detected.

Shelter and food were the next concerns, but the radio might solve much of that. Night would be coming quickly here in the high mountains, and with it bitter cold.

He felt her arctic gear. Nearly dry. His then. It was nearly dry as well. Soon, very soon, dry enough that body warmth would do the rest.

Light would be critical to evaluate and possibly diagnose, then repair one of the radios if repair were in order. But perhaps it was only a problem of range, or some Russian jamming. He couldn't be sure. The differences between these helmet radios and any radios he had extensively worked with five centuries before was analogous to the differences between a personal computer unit and one of the giant defense department mainframes he had seen, the complication and sophistication so vastly greater. Given time, he was confident he could deduce the nature of the problem and, if it were correctable, correct it. It had to be something related to the helmets taking the dousing they had. It was the only commonality that might explain why both helmet radios would not function. If not that, then a problem of range or Soviet jamming. The former he might correct. The latter was beyond his control.

He looked around him. Rocky. Barren of vegetation. No caves evident and no depressions of suitable size for a protracted stay.

It was clear that their first order of business was to move on to a more suitable location.

"Damn the thing," John Rourke almost whispered, replacing the guts of the radio in the helmet in reverse order to his removal of it.

From his musette bag, Rourke removed a small tool, unfolding the screwdriver blade of closest appropriate size. He had already cleaned the twin stainless Detonics .45s, leaving the more difficult job of cleaning the N-Frame Smith & Wesson revolver until last. Carefully, after verifying its empty condition, he removed the crane screw, forwardmost of the sideplate screws, setting it down on a smooth rock near him, then opening the cylinder and sliding cylinder and crane off the frame. He set them aside, then using the same screwdriver bit removed the two remaining screws in the sideplate. Using the haft of the Life Support System X knife, wrapped in his bandanna handkerchief, he tapped the frame and dislodged the sideplate, lifting it free of the frame.

The lockwork showed accumulated moisture. Meticulously, he began to disassemble it, setting out the small parts in the order in which he removed them.

There was no time to make a proper bellows, nor were there appropriate materials readily at hand. He removed the face shield from his riding helmet and used the shield as a fan to force hot air to the interior of the frame after first using the bandanna to dry out obvious moisture.

His thighs were covered with gooseflesh, but his Levi's weren't yet dry. He kept working, his hands shaking a little with the cold.

The German replication of the Break-Free CLP lubricant he applied to the inner surface of the frame, to the small parts. He reassembled the lockwork, then carefully replaced the sideplate, replacing two of the screws as well.

He removed the cylinder from the crane, unscrewed the tip of the base pin/ejector rod, and removed the star ejector.

If Natalia could be made to walk, he judged they could make it perhaps as far as three miles down before she would be exhausted. Within another mile or so, there would be trees. That meant easily fabricated shelter. He reassembled the parts, slid the crane back into the frame and closed the cylinder, then turned in the third and final screw. He began replacing the Pachmayr grips.

The ammunition he had he would have to trust until proven otherwise. If the specifications derived from analysis of the federal 185-grain JHP .45s and 180-grain JHP .44 Magnums were followed to the letter when the Germans had fabricated these lots, he would assume the ammunition reliable despite the dousing in the river. He hoped.

He returned to the river, still trouserless, washed his hands of the oil and powder residues with sand and water. Across the river, war raged. Somewhere across the river, Michael and Annie and Paul and the others had to have survived.

To take Natalia back into the river was unthinkable. And at any event, there was no likely place to cross safely. Downriver, perhaps a natural crossing point existed or a bridge of some sort could be fabricated.

And, once across the river, they would only be nearer to the battle between the Russians and the Chinese of the Second City.

Rourke stood to his full height, as he continued planning commencing a light routine of calisthenics to heighten muscle tone and circulation. He was beginning to feel warmer, and his clothes would be adequately dried soon.

Han Lu Chen spoke of wolves set loose by the Chinese of the Second City, but Rourke considered them more likely to be large feral dogs. And, if such a population survived, the Chinese had to have released other animals upon which these wolf-like canines could feed. Rabbits and other small game, perhaps game as large as deer, might be found. The thing to do, of course, was find the tracks of the feral dogs and assume that their range took them near the most abundant game population. In the lower elevations there would be edible plants until he could find meat, if this lasted that long.

He walked back from the river's edge, squatted on the end of the arctic parkas he had thrown over Natalia and took his socks from near the fire. Stiff, but warm and dry. He rubbed them in his hands to relax the fiber content and wiped the soles of his feet clean, then put them on.

The jeans were slightly damp near the seams, but otherwise satisfactorily dry. He skinned into them. His boots and belts and holsters he had attended to earlier, utilizing the leather dressing compound from his musette bag. He got into his boots, feeling warmer already.

He threaded on his belt, a one and three-quarter-inch 11-12 ounce cowhide strap, like his gunbelt and holster originally produced for him before the Night of the War by Milt Sparks. He secured the Sparks Six-Pack and the sheath for the Crain LS-X and finished threading, closing the solid brass Garrison-style buckle.

He looked at Natalia. She was sleeping, but had to be awakened.

Rourke holstered the Model 629 Smith & Wesson, securing the six-inch in the full flap holster. It was a fine revolver, but would never have the feel of the Python which had been mutilated on the rocks beneath the Retreat. Someday, Rourke promised himself, he would restore the Python, carry it once again.

He picked up his parka and pulled it on over the double

Alessi rig in which Rourke habitually carried the little Detonics .45s.

Rourke dropped to his knees beside her. "Natalia—wake up, now."

Her eyes opened, so suddenly, with so startled a look in them that for an instant she reminded him more of a wild animal. She said nothing, only stared at him. "You'll have to get dressed. We have to walk on a little while and then you can rest again. All of your clothes are dry."

He reached beside the fire and took her underwear for her, putting it under the covers for her. She made no move to put anything on. "Natalia? Please?"

But she wasn't even looking at him, was looking through him as though he weren't there. And, Rourke thought, perhaps to her he wasn't. "You must get dressed. You have to. I left you my nice gray woolen sweater. Remember you said it always looked so warm? Well, it's just for you now. You can wear it and be warm. I've had it very close to the fire for a long time. It'll keep you warm, Natalia."

She only stared.

Slowly—but she offered no resistance—he drew back her parka, draped over her, and the emergency thermal blanket that was beneath it.

He had seen her naked body several times, held her body beside him to warm her, undressed her to dry her clothing. But he realized he was staring at her. She made no natural movement to cover her bare breasts, to conceal the triangle of hair below the firm concavity of her abdomen. He wondered suddenly how she had looked in the days before she had grown too tall for the ballet, how she had looked perhaps performing something like *Swan Lake*. The long, slender legs, so beautifully shaped— John Rourke closed his eyes tightly, his hands on her bare shoulders. "Natalia," he whispered.

But as he opened his eyes, her gaze remained unchanged.

John Rourke picked up the silk undergarment Natalia had worn. He searched his mind for what it was called—a "teddy"?

It was trimmed subtly with lace and seemed more fragile than logic dictated it really was. He supposed, almost mechanically, that if he had gotten her out of it, he could get her back into it somehow. His fingers felt ten times too large for his hands as he began to try . . .


Michael Rourke opened his eyes and instantly regretted it for the pain it caused in his head, but reopened his eyes because of the happiness he felt. That he was alive was obvious, unless the afterlife had a cold climate as well. The source of his happiness was in the face that looked so lovingly down on his: Maria Leuden's face, her auburn hair tossed over the lowered hood of her parka, her gray-green eyes (the color of his mother's eyes) soft and beautiful behind the lenses of her wire-rimmed glasses.

"Michael?"

"Hi."

"Michael!"

"Shh—my head hurts. Just kiss me."

She leaned over him, her lips coming against his mouth, and his hands grasped her shoulders.

"Michael—" As he held her, he thought she might be crying.

# Chapter Seven

She had awakened in the middle of the night. Her nightgown was damp. By the light of a candle, she saw the color and knew the reason for the wetness. The rest of the night, she could not sleep. One life was ending.

In the morning, she quietly whispered the secret to her mother. Her mother began to cry. Her father was told to take her brother and leave their domiciliary unit. Her mother bathed her, fondled her lovingly, cried more.

It was the day when her first menstrual cycle began and when new life began; pledged from birth to fulfill a sacred destiny as a Maiden of the Sun, she was taken, wearing her clean dress, to the temple. Her mother, slump-shouldered, merely walked away.

Never after three days prior to her eleventh birthday did she see mother or father or sister or brother. Sisters were her family, the high priestess most important among them, the Perfect One her mother, the god her father and life-giver.

There was ritual to learn, and much of ritual was obedience, to the god, of course, but through his Perfect One and then through the high priestess, distilled through the elder of her new sisters.

She would cook, she would clean, she would, after fear and screaming proved to no avail, submit to the beatings which were to build her character. And each morning and each evening, she would cast off the gray dress of her labors and clothe her body in the white robe of the Maidens and serve her god. It was only after some years that she realized that the menial tasks through which she worked, the brutalization administered by those senior to her—that all of this too served her god.

Some of the other girls would giggle as they spoke about the god, that his earthly appearance dictated that they be virgins. It was some time before she apprehended this, and only because she remembered her younger brothers from the family she had belonged to before but belonged to no longer. Was this why they worshipped the god and no man of any kind could come near to them? Would, someday, his mystic power in all its greatness enter her?

In matters religious, hers was now the ultimate authority and publicly recognized as being supreme to that of Mao. Privately, her word was supreme in all matters, Mao worshipping at her body as she once had worshipped before her god. Her god had never entered her, but Mao had. And Mao had proven much less than a god.

Now her chief priestess bowed before her. A cloud of mortar particles, fine and tan and dusty-smelling, drifted down from the ceiling above them as one of the explosions rumbled from without the confines of the temple.

The Maidens of the Sun, long black hair cascading past narrow waists and virginally rounded hips, stood, eyes lowered, hands folded in prayer, in a semi-circle arced behind the priestess. As one, they fell to their knees and extended their supple young bodies over the cold stones of the floor, arms outstretched at their sides, legs locked as tightly together as if they were bound, warm, cherry red lips caressing cold gray stone. How many times had she formed her body into the shape of a cross and kissed the stone? And when the cross had been asymmetrical, her legs had been bound and she had been forced to spend the period between the lowering and rising there on the floor to practice her humility. How many times?

And, at last, she had been called before the Perfect One,

47

shown her dexterity at the altar, recited the Sacred Names, been anointed the high priestess. She would practice at the altar's keyboard for hours each day, reciting the Sacred Names as she tapped out the Holy Symbols which so wondrously formed them. The Sun gave them this power and in the darkness this power was taken from them.

How many times had she prostrated herself before her god? She had never counted, although she had counted the days which had become months and the months which had become years until that one blissful moment when the Perfect One had been vulnerable. It was wrong, but it was so terribly right. The Perfect One was not perfect. The very vulnerability of the Perfect One revealed that and was, perhaps, truly a sign.

Vulnerable.

And alone.

Dead.

And, ever after, she was the Perfect One.

She stood. "That which we worship which is one with our god must be readied that our holy city and the wrath of our god may be immortalized and whosoever does not believe in his power will forever be vanquished."

She had worshipped in the service of the Sun for more than an entire decade, had attained the age of nineteen before she had realized the nature of the deity she served. In the forbidden books known only to the Perfect One, hers to read when she became the Perfect One.

Her god was, indeed, the Sun. In all his fiery majesty.

Fallen on their faces, prostrate before him, the Maidens began their mantra, and with a sincerity she had felt not at all throughout the third decade of her life which, like all life, was now coming to a close, she turned, dropped to her knees, prostrated herself before her god and began the recitation, the Sacred Names which the high priestess, second among mortals only to her, would draw out in the Holy Symbols with the altar keys.

Click . . . click . . . click . . .

The fingers of the high priestess tapped out the Holy Symbols which so intricately, so precisely formed the Sacred Names.

And then the god spoke, his voice vibrating through her very soul. His words were like none other in their majesty. And he revealed to them a Sacred Name of power. "Thermonuclear Warhead System Fourteen, Type Three, Battery Twenty-Nine is armed. Countdown commences."

The rapture of union with her god would soon be upon them.

# Chapter Eight

Michael Rourke heard the voice of his friend Han Lu Chen and opened his eyes. The headache instantly returned. But he squinted his eyes tight against it so he could still see. His sister, Annie, was standing over him, and he found himself starting to laugh at her. It was so odd seeing his always femininely attired sister in trousers. Han was saying, "The battle is spreading outward and nearing us. The forces of the Second City are hurtling themselves at the Soviet ground forces. It will do no good, of course."

Annie started to speak, but then Michael heard another voice. It was that of Vassily Prokopiev, the KGB major, new commander of the KGB Elite Corps. "I would say that the wisest and best thing for all of you would be to place yourselves voluntarily in the hands of my forces. I could guarantee safe conduct in return for the way all of you have cared for me, risked your lives for me, your brother most of all, Mrs. Rubenstein. But as what we have come to call 'The Rourke Family,' you are all marked for death, or worse. I cannot guarantee safe conduct, no matter how much, personally, I would like to do so."

"I know that, Major," Annie responded. "When we move on, we can aim you in the right direction, perhaps—"

"You would be fools to do so. I might make a valuable hostage—and certainly a willing one. That is the least I can offer. And should we encounter the Chinese of this Second

City, I can fight—well."

Michael Rourke turned his head with some difficulty—the pain. "You're an honest man, Vassily."

"Michael!" Annie's voice. She dropped to her knees beside him, her hands cradling his face.

"I'm fine—I think. But God, have I got a headache."

In the next moment, Maria Leuden knelt beside him, leaning over him, her hair touching his cheek, her lips touching his forehead. "Ohh, Michael—"

He held her hand, his other arm enfolding Annie against him.

"You are a resilient man, Michael Rourke," the Russian said, almost laughing.

"Part of being a Rourke." Michael smiled. "What's happening—"

"Welcome back to the living. I must resume my post," Han Lu Chen—he was dressed like a Mongol—offered, making a soft salute and disappearing out of Michael's peripheral vision.

"Where's—"

"Paul and Otto are out looking for Daddy and Natalia," Annie said abruptly, sitting up, putting her hands to her hair, just holding them there at her neck. "They've been out of radio contact ever since we all split up—"

"What—"

"You were hit with a sword," Annie volunteered.

Michael released Maria's hand and touched at the bandage on the side of his head. "Wonderful. My guns—did—"

"Han got all your weapons for you when he agreed to be your executioner, remember?"

Michael started to nod, realized the mistake too late and winced at the pain in his head, closing his eyes tight against it. "Right— Dad and Natalia— What, ahh—"

"Doctor Rourke and Major Tiemerovna," Prokopiev began, "were separated from the rest of us. They were pursued. They have not been seen or heard from since. That is my understanding."

"Paul and Otto are looking for them," Annie concluded. "I can contact them—Paul and Otto—by radio."

"I need to sit up—and where are my guns?" Michael sat up and felt as if he would die. The next step would be standing, so he told himself that would probably be worse . . .


Natalia could not walk unaided. She walked, but she walked without purpose, wandered, and here, in the high rocks down through which they climbed, to take a false step might be fatal. Rourke alternated holding her hand or her elbow as they moved, Natalia from time to time, mantra-like, chanting his name, at times a haunting smile crossing her lips, as if she were dreaming of something pleasant yet totally awake.

The grazing wound he'd sustained to his right arm made the arm feel stiff at times, but there was no real pain. The weight of his weapons combined with hers—he no longer trusted her with anything with which she might do herself harm—was considerable. Added to his twin Detonics mini-guns and the two Scoremasters and the 629, her L-Frame Smith .357s and her suppressor-fitted Walther PPK/S, his knives and hers was the weight of the helmets which he could not abandon because of their integral radio sets which might be the only means of extraction for them.

They kept moving.

"John . . . John . . . John . . ."

"I'm here. How could I leave you?"

"John . . . John . . ."

"You'll only make yourself hoarse. Please—let's be quiet together. It's beautiful here." Gunfire and explosions rumbled in the distance. "We're just going for a walk. Hold on to my hand."

"John . . ."

"I'm here, Natalia."

# Chapter Nine

"Report coming in now from Hekla, Comrade Colonel."

"Read it back to me, Corporal."

"Yes, Comrade Colonel—'Headquarters Command Code Orange. Operation Storm, Sigma Sector. Advancing against Hekla Cone. Heavy fighting at enemy base outside Cone. Aggregate loss of personnel and equipment thirteen percent over estimate. Continuing advance. Need more air support.'—"

"All right—try to get him his air support," Antonovitch hissed, passing through the communications control center as quickly as he could now before another message arrived. It was going as he had expected, the casualty rates higher than anticipated but as yet not unacceptable.

He passed through the air lock of the hermetically sealed tent and into the cold late afternoon air, no coat, only his uniform blouse and the shirt beneath it. He ran his fingers back through his hair.

The one he wanted to hear from he had not heard from— Nikita Achinski. Once Achinski had attained his objective, then all the madness would stop and victory would be at hand.

He felt more than heard anything from behind him, turned abruptly toward the communications tent and saw the usually somber face of his adjutant. "Comrade Colonel! Achinski reports a major element of the enemy land forces destroyed, their lines of reinforcement and supply broken—he is advancing on the Second Chinese City, Comrade Colonel!"

"The missiles? Any word of these?"

"No mention, Comrade Colonel—I can recontact—"

"No—not yet. Let him go on." If only, Antonovitch almost verbalized, Prokopiev had not been lost . . .


The muscles around the reduced shoulder dislocation hurt far more than the flesh around the gunshot wound to his other shoulder.

Why had Michael Rourke saved his life, Prokopiev asked himself for the hundredth time, perhaps the thousandth time?

The name of Rourke was one used to frighten the small children of the Underground City, a terrorist and murderer. Was Michael the son of such a man? Was the very beautiful, very sensitive-seeming Annie the daughter of such a man? And the Jew, Rubenstein, husband of Rourke's daughter—why would such a man of obvious bravery and goodness be so devoted to a man such as John Rourke?

The facts seemed evident. Rourke was an enemy, but a noble one. All Rourkes were enemies, but noble enemies. The rest of what he had been taught to believe was a convenient lie. Lies, of course, were the bulwark of statecraft. And official lies such as this were policy. Policy was to be unquestioned. He would not question the lie, just realize from now until his life ended—which would not be very long, he surmised—that the lie was not to be believed.

This clear in his mind, Vassily Prokopiev began the complex process of sorting out his options.

John Rourke was a war criminal, but as a commando of the Elite Corps, his job was not to seek out war criminals. Yet, as its commander (unless his death was assumed and he was replaced, also likely), his directive was the welfare of the State, which dictated, of course, that John Rourke and all the Rourke family must die. Yet John Rourke was, in all likelihood, dead. As to the rest, circumstance had made them comrades. And all

54

his life he had been taught that loyalty to one's comrade was second only to one's loyalty to the State. At the moment, the State was an abstraction, his comrades were real.

He had read many suppressed books, in one finding a curious reference to a man named Sartre and a concept labeled "situation ethics." Prokopiev realized that he was, after all, the living proof that such books were dangerous to the unwitting reader.

# Chapter Ten

Snow was falling heavily in the lower elevations and, as they had pressed on throughout the waning daylight hours, they penetrated more deeply into the storm. With the cover of the snowfall, it would be less likely they could be spotted from the air by the Soviet airpower. With no radiation detection equipment available to him, it would be safer to melt snow for water than avail himself of the local water supply, albeit that a bushel's worth of snow was needed to produce a pint of drinking water. With the lack of appropriate shelter materials and the coming of the colder temperatures of the night, the snow would serve as insulation and artificially elevate the temperature, and could possibly be utilized to insulate what shelter he would fabricate.

He left Natalia in a niche of rocks protected from the wind, wrapping her in the blanket, half tempted to leave his parka over her as well. But reason prevailed over emotion—should he become ill, her chances of survival in her present state would be zero.

The snow fell in large flakes which clung to his eyelashes and his hair, the hood down, the skin of his cheeks tingling with the cold, but his body warm from exercise.

John Rourke's right fist clenched the haft of the Life Support System X, handmade for him five centuries before by the Weatherford, Texas knifemaker Jack Crain. He brought the primary edge down against the base of the five-foot pine tree's trunk, then once more and finally a third time, toppling the fir easily, heaving it into the pile with others he had already cut.

The pine trees, abundant here, would suffice to form the bare necessities upon which he could expand.

He didn't resheath the LS-X knife, because of the pine tar on the blade that would have to be removed.

As he began hauling the trees toward the site he had picked for their shelter, he realized the snow was falling more rapidly, more heavily . . .

Michael Rourke, brushing the snow from his eyes, squinted down into a depression where perhaps centuries ago a river had run, below the rocks in which he and Annie now lay side-by-side. Men and equipment—Chinese, but from the Second City—were moving downward along its course. Annie was speaking into her helmet radio, although she did not wear the helmet. "Paul—we have a concentration of troops from the Second City closing in our direction. We may have to evacuate this position. Any word on Daddy? Over."

Faintly, just well enough to be intelligible, Michael could hear Paul Rubenstein's response. "There's no sign of them ever having been in this vicinity. We're crossing the river at the earliest opportunity. Snowing there too? Over?"

"Yes—very heavily. Don't cross the river—you could—"

The radios were constructed so that sending and receiving was done on separate bands and hence it was possible to interrupt a transmission. "We have to. If they're in trouble, with this snowfall it will only make things worse for them. We'll be out of radio contact in another few miles. We'll need a rendezvous. Over."

"I know you have to do what you think is best. But how—"

"We need a rendezvous," Paul interrupted again. "Have Michael check your map. I'm thinking of G-7 on the revised grid your dad made over the German maps. The prominent

57

feature—I don't want to get more specific in case we're being monitored."

Already, Michael was folding the topographic map into the proper segment. There was a structure atop a plateau of modest elevation, the river running past it in a lazy snake shape. "Tell him I see the spot. Set a time, Annie."

"Paul—Michael has the location pinpointed." She was looking over Michael's shoulder now. "When? Over."

"Twenty-four to thirty-six hours from now is the latest we'll be. Over."

"That's too long—if the Russians knock out the Second City, there should be scattering Chinese troops all over the area, not to mention the Russians themselves. Over."

"Twenty-four hours then. I need that. Over."

"Affirmative on that. I love you. Tell Otto to be careful, too. And find Daddy and Natalia."

"I will, sweetheart," Paul's voice came back. "Out."

Michael Rourke looked into his sister's eyes. They were tear-rimmed. "I'm really afraid," she whispered, her voice breaking a little.

"I know that. So am I. But if anybody can do it, Paul can. And as soon as we reach the rendezvous, you and Maria can keep an eye on Prokopiev and Han and I can join the search." Michael Rourke's eyes were drawn back into the gulch below them and the Chinese forces—withdrawing or moving into some new strategic posture?

"Damn," he hissed.

# Chapter Eleven

From the bark of one of the larger pines he had ventured deeper into the treeline to topple then had, with some difficulty, taken the main trunk out with him, over his shoulder, John Rourke cut several large pieces. As he walked out, he checked the fresh snow for signs of rabbit or anything larger, remembering once again the tales told by Han Lu Chen of the Chinese wolves. Tracks of woodrats and mice could be seen occasionally, but nothing he looked forward to eating. It was hard to imagine that the Chinese of the Second City had saved such humble creatures throughout the centuries for release into the wild by design, so he pre-supposed poor management instead.

But there was no sign of larger animal life.

Confident that he had enough bark to satisfy his perceived needs, Rourke pushed one end of the log—shorter in length than half a telephone pole but nearly the girth—into the fire he had built just outside one end of the shelter he had fabricated of pine boughs and bared branches. The tree trunk began to catch with the aid of fat lighter he had gathered from nearby pines earlier and with which he started the fire originally. It was crystallized pine tar, one of nature's great combustibles. Rather than utilizing a match, since these might be precious later, and his Zippo so soaked that it would not light, he had made a bow-shaped fire-starter aided with magnesium shavings from the stick of magnesium he carried in his musette bag.

Natalia still rested. With a flaming ember, John Rourke lit a cigar, this one of the ones in the waterproof case he carried in the musette bag as well. It was warm enough beneath the pine bough shelter that he had removed his coat, and he rolled up his shirtsleeves as he set to work with the bark. The old woodsman's method had been open to him, but he had never liked it. To boil water by hollowing out a segment of log, then fire-heating stones and applying them with improvised tongs to a container of water until the temperature was elevated to the boiling point had always struck him as doubling the work, and at any event it was necessary to avoid stones which would either burst or turn to slivers when quenched in the cold water. And his greatest problem was the water itself, since he was utilizing snow. He began roasting some of his materials over the stone-encircled fire, whittling with the Crain knife on small pegs of pine.

And the former method presupposed a kettle of some sort in which to heat the water. Instead, he opted for the more esoteric, yet, to his reckoning, practical method, making a kettle and simply heating it with the existing fire. For this, he needed the thinner inner bark of the tree which he had worked to separate from the coarser, uneven outer bark, using the Crain LS-X. After some careful cutting, he had a roughly square sheet, nearly twelve inches on a side, which was roasted to the point now where it had become suitably malleable. Folding the opposing corners together to form a triangle at the newly formed apex, he folded once again. Eyeing the creases carefully, Rourke turned the bark section over, then began the next sequence of folds. Now folding along the scribed lines made by the folds, he formed overlapping corners, securing them with one of the suitably sized slivers of pine he had previously sharpened to have points at one end. He did the same with the other set of corners, forming a box-shaped object under six inches square and less than four inches deep.

He had constructed the fire with an eye toward the kettle, and the most important factor to remember in its use was that the flame could only contact that portion of the kettle where there was actually liquid. If it touched the sides, the kettle would burn. He set the kettle into the snow beside the fire, then proceeded to pack snowballs, impaling these on forked branches scavenged from the fabrication of their shelter, then allowed these snowballs, near the heat, to melt into the kettle. It was a tedious process, but necessary. Once there was a sufficient amount of water that he could leave a residue in the pot, it would be simpler.

While the snowballs melted, he began working other sheets of bark into needed utensils, namely a drinking cup and a water bucket. He had taught Michael and Annie, years ago, how to make such items, although Annie had been quite young. After he awakened them from the Sleep and before he himself returned to it, he retaught such skills. Annie had seemed particularly fascinated with the crafting of a folding bark cup (they had used paper, more abundant there near the Retreat and just as useful, even to use as a kettle). Little better than half the size needed for a kettle, the method was basically similar, the volume of the cup approximately one-quarter pint, or as he had explained it to them when they were little, half as much as a school milk carton. The cup was easily folded and could be closed against dirt from the pocket.

A sufficient quantity of snow had melted and Rourke began heating it on flat stones over the fire with a small gap through which the flame could reach only the base of the kettle, reducing the likelihood of burning to zero. As the water warmed, he added more snow, melting more snowballs into the bucket for future use.

He began working with the remaining bark, grinding it with stones into something the consistency of rough flour. He gradually added melted snow until it became sufficiently doughlike that he could form it into crudely shaped tortilla-like sheets. He placed them aside for later cooking.

A glance by the firelight at the black face of his Rolex told him it was about time to check the few crude traps he had laid earlier when he had gone into the woods for the larger tree. Adding more of the snowball drippings to his kettle, edging the log farther in, he was confident the fire was still low enough that he didn't have to worry about total evaporation even if the water should begin to boil.

Rourke checked Natalia, her condition unchanged, seized by a deep and restless sleep from which he prayed she would awaken restored—but he knew that she would not, barring miraculous intervention.

Rourke rolled down his sleeves, donned his coat and picked up his knife, then passed the primary edge through the flames several times quickly, to burn off the pine tar, which was highly flammable, the steel not in the fire long enough to affect temper. He used a snowball to wipe it clean, then dried it on his trouser leg, resheathing. He gathered up several of the longer shavings from his all-purpose tree for use in short-term emergency lighting should such prove necessary.

Quickly, Rourke left the shelter, moving through the deep snow now toward his self-styled trapline. If the snow persisted, by morning he would need to fabricate snowshoes, most suitable the tailless bearpaw design considering the mountainous terrain, their blunt toe shape useful in kicking to form a step in the snow. They were the simplest to use and John Rourke hadn't been on snowshoes since the pursuit of his daughter and her kidnapper to Iceland months ago, and before that for five centuries.

He slogged onward, moving deeper into the trees in the gathering darkness, mindful of the fact that his flashlight still worked but unwilling to waste battery power until and unless it were needed.

Perhaps three hundred yards from the shelter, John Rourke stopped, frozen in his tracks by a sound he had not heard in five centuries. So much for Chinese wolves, he thought: these were feral dogs.

The sound of the dogs was between him and the hut. And

although the fire was essentially sheltered from aerial observation (by design), it would be visible when approaching from ground level. It would keep the creatures away from the hut, perhaps driving them toward him.

His mind raced. Hunting? Perhaps, or fleeing the war between Russians and Second City Chinese, perhaps both? No tracks had shown such creatures in the nearby area earlier. A gunshot in these woods would be heard for miles, might be just enough to draw the attention of stray enemy forces, and with two enemies, double the chances of that.

John Rourke unsheathed the Life Support System X. He looked quickly to right and left, then crouched and brought the twelve-inch Bowie-patterned blade down quickly against a sapling perhaps three feet in height, the sounds of the animals getting closer. With the LS-X he quickly chopped off the boughs, then stabbed the Crain knife into a nearby trunk. He reached under his coat, to the small of his back where he carried the little A.G. Russell Sting IA Black Chrome sheathed. He drew it out, fitted it to the base of the boughless pine, then drew the long, thin shavings from his pocket, his musette bag with his spare bootlaces back at the shelter. Quickly, but as stoutly as time allowed, Rourke bound the Sting IA to the shaft of the sapling, the howling and yelping blood-curdlingly close now. The improvised flexible spear in his right hand, he snatched the LS-X with his left, then withdrew into deeper treecover. What would slow his movement would slow theirs, what might all but discourage him might very well discourage them, unless they were very hungry indeed.

And then he saw twin balls of fire looking toward him, growing in immensity, moving through the gray fog of dusk and swirling snow.

Feral dogs, indeed, but as lupine in appearance as any true wolf he had seen.

Coming, then another pair of eyes, the first pair's body members and torso taking shape, then a third pair of eyes, the first pair's attendant form now fully defined. Rourke edged back. If it would be life or death, he would use a gun, but it would have to be that.

Three more materialized through the snow, making six in all. They were coming for him. He wondered if they smelled the same fear he smelled, which was his own.

Coming.

John Rourke moved as the pack leader, larger, as anticipated, sniffed at the snowy ground, as if scenting something which wasn't properly there but seemed to be there all the same. And then the creature wheeled directly toward him, fewer than a dozen yards away.

Rourke's right hand tightened on the shaft of the makeshift spear.

The creature lunged, Rourke's right arm upthrusting, the Sting IA that was the point of his weapon penetrating the creature beneath the sternum, the animal's own weight carrying the blade through to rip open the abdominal cavity, Rourke ducking left and down, rolling, the feral beast's body tumbling into the snow inches from where Rourke had stood, the spear shaft gone now, the animal rolling in agony.

The second of the wolves lunged for him, Rourke's right hand going for the 629. As the animal's arc of motion brought him within reach, Rourke's right arm arced outward, backhanding the six-inch piece of stainless steel pipe which was the revolver's barrel across the animal's face. Rourke wheeled right, made a saber thrust with the Crain knife, in and withdrawn as the animal yelped in agony and fell.

A blur of motion. He saw it, reacted, then felt the impact and smelled the odor as a third animal's body crashed against his own. It was on him, Rourke's right hand moving, ramming the muzzle of the revolver into the gaping wound of a mouth, no way to use the knife properly, but instead crashing the skull-crusher that was formed out of the double buttcap at the base of the pommel into the right side of the animal's head,

Rourke's right knee smashing up into the trunk.

The animal rolled away, Rourke to his feet, wheeling half right, as the animal made to lunge again, Rourke's left leg snapping up and out, the toe of his left combat boot impacting the apex of the animal's drooling muzzle, sending it rolling away into the trees, yelping maddeningly.

The fourth animal and the fifth were coming for him, Rourke thrusting with the LS-X, catching one of the creatures in the torso and gutting it, averting his face as the spray of blood started. The fifth animal was on him and Rourke stumbled back, falling, the animal's jaws snapping over his left arm, but catching clothing, not flesh—this time. Before it could bite again, Rourke crashed the butt of the 629 down over its skull, between the eyes, then as he was able to move his left arm, rammed the knife in through the right side of the creature's neck.

Rourke was on his knees, the blood-dripping Crain knife balled tight in his left fist, the revolver in his right. The sixth wolflike dog—where was it?

Suddenly his breath was gone and he was gasping, falling, the revolver spilling from his right hand, the knife slipping away between the fingers of his left. The creature rolled over him, Rourke looking up just in time to see it impact, roll, then twist upward and lunge. John Rourke, choking, eyes tearing, scooped two handfuls of snow and flung them toward the animal's face as he forced himself to his knees, then fell away left. The creature's concentration seemed broken for only seconds. And as the animal came for him, Rourke bent forward, shrugging his parka from his shoulders, flinging it over the animal and blanketing the creature with it for an instant. His hands reached to the double Alessi rig, but grabbed at the harness halves instead of the twin stainless Detonics pistols the holsters themselves held.

As the animal shook itself free of the coat, Rourke was on it, praying the harness coupling would hold, looping it over the creature's head, then throwing his body weight back and left, the animal snarling, yelping, then a cracking sound so loud that it was almost ear-splitting—the neck—and then all effort against Rourke subsided.

John Rourke fell forward, face down into the snow.

Six.

On hands and knees, his right fist still clenched to his shoulder harness, he looked around him as much as the dying light would allow.

None of the animals seemed particularly weighty—lucky for him, Rourke smiled—but it would be easy enough to make a quick post-mortem and separate the healthiest of the pack.

The explorers Lewis and Clark had survived for a time on dog meat and, though Rourke had never tasted it, he'd worked with men all over the world who had, at one time or another, thrived on it. If nothing else, the hearts.

He stood up, inspecting his shoulder holster as best he could in the fading light, finding it none the worse for wear, shrugging into it, checking that both .45s were secure. His coat was another matter. Much of the left sleeve was in shreds. He had needle and thread and could adequately repair it.

The 629 would need a barrel-swabbing again. He wiped it clean with snow, dried it on the outside of his coat and holstered it.

His little A.G. Russell knife. It lay only a yard from his feet, still partially attached to a stump of pine sapling shaft.

He picked it up, began to clean it with snow.

It would not be good for Natalia to know what they were eating, but— He sheathed the Sting. John Rourke spotted the Crain LS-X on the ground and picked it up, mechanically wiping the blade with handfuls of snow. There was a school of thought which held that long-bladed, seriously proportioned knives were less than practical, merely for show. He smiled, finding himself wondering how many of those adherents to that philosophy had found themselves confronted by six hungry wild animals when the use of a gun was all but out of the question.

He shrugged.

On the negative side, what he contemplated made for a more than mildly disgusting proposition, but on the plus side his exertions had worked up a healthy appetite. He began inspecting the provender providence had brought them.

# Chapter Twelve

She twirled once in front of the mirror, the silk skirts of the almost midnight-blue dress she wore ballooning outward from her ankles, the glass slippers on her feet catching the firelight and sparkling to rival the diamonds at her throat, her ears, her wrists, all but the diamond on the third finger of her left hand which was at once enormous yet tasteful, beautiful.

She heard his footsteps along the tiled wooden floor behind her and felt her heart skip a beat, saw his image in the mirror and felt her cheeks flush.

Natalia turned toward him so abruptly that the fabric of her dress rustled.

"Hello."

His voice was as one imagined the voice of God might sound, but too human, in a single word saying more to her than any man had ever begun to express in ten thousand.

His left hand reached out to her, beneath the french cuff of his shirt the simple elegance of his stainless steel Rolex wristwatch catching the firelight as well. His fingers stroked gently at the bareness of her neck, found a loosened lock by the nape, entwined gently in it and she bent her face to his wrist, her lips softly caressing the strength that was his hands.

He took a step back from her, shrugging his massive shoulders so slightly that she would not have noticed had not her eyes been in thrall to his every movement. Her hands touched the black butterfly bow which emerged from the white collar of his shirt, the black pearl studs of his shirtfront rising and falling gently as he breathed.

He took her into his arms, the texture of his tuxedo wonderfully rough feeling against her bare chest and arms and shoulders, her breasts pressing against the fabric of her bodice, tight against him.

"I love you," he told her.

But she knew that.

John Rourke bent his face over hers and his lips parted. She closed her eyes.

The floor beneath them seemed to rise up.

There was gunfire and the sounds of explosive devices were everywhere.

Her eyes were open, but still she couldn't see him. "John! John! John . . . John . . ." The fire which had cast its warm glow over the ballroom where she had waited for him—how long?—now consumed the ballroom and she was surrounded by it and she bunched her dress tight around her as she dropped to her knees, huddling there as the fires rose in yellow walls around her. "John!" Her ring—it was not a diamond, yet it was, but it was no logner blue or white, but blood-red like a ruby and she screamed for him until the heat invaded her lungs, her arms folding over her breasts, the heat searing her flesh. "John . . . John . . . John . . ." Why didn't he come for her . . .

John Rourke touched his left hand to her neck, raising her head just a little as he told her, "This is really good-tasting. I amazed myself. Kind of a stew. Neither of us has really eaten in almost twenty-four hours and we both need some nourishment." He had par-boiled the flesh just to be on the safe side. "This will taste good. A little hot but that'll warm you up inside. You'll be feeling better in no time. And at any minute now, I expect Annie and Paul to come rolling up. Annie'll get you feeling your old self, Natalia. When she was a little girl and

I was very tired or depressed, I'd help tuck her in at night and get her to give me a kiss and then a hug and have her pat me on the shoulder or the back. She started it, one time when she knew things weren't going right, somehow. And it made me feel better, so we started kidding about it and I'd say, 'Now give me a pat so I feel good,' and she'd give me a pat. And the funny thing was that it always made me feel better. So, when Annie gets here, you tell her you want her to give you a big hug and then a pat. And don't forget the part about the pat, because that's important. But you've got to eat so you'll feel strong again."

Slowly, with greater difficulty than he'd ever had feeding the children when they were little, he fed her, with the bark spoon he'd made catching at the bits of food as they dribbled from her mouth. She had dirtied herself while he'd been gone and he'd bathed her as necessary, covered her. After she was fed, he would have to wash out her things, dry them by the fire.

Was she going down?

Throughout the day, with his reminding her, she had cared for her own bodily functions. He told himself that it was just that she had been sleeping too soundly and in her exhausted and confused state—

"Natalia!" His throat ached with her name.

# Chapter Thirteen

Russian helicopters were ringing the Second Chinese City. Fuel to burn, Michael Rourke surmised, just like the Second City. Fires dotted the mountainside into which it had been built, heavy fighting by all the defensive positions.

Their movement throughout the late afternoon and into the early evening, until the snow became too heavy to travel without lights, had taken them along the base of a high ridge and, because there was no choice, closer to the beleaguered Second City.

With Annie and Maria Leuden flanking him despite his protests, Michael Rourke had climbed the ridge to assay the condition of the battle.

Maria, close beside him, spoke softly as she said, "In ancient times, it was not unknown for persons whose options had been entirely exhausted to risk destruction of self in order to defeat an enemy."

"You mean their nuclear weapons," Annie interjected. "Don't you?"

"Yes." Maria nodded.

Michael Rourke looked from Maria to his sister. "You think they'd detonate a nuclear weapon to—"

"Maybe they'd detonate them all. I mean, it would only take one if it were set off properly, wouldn't it?"

"I don't know, Annie," Michael told her, shaking his head

despairingly. "Yeah—maybe. Probably. Shit—"

He started back down from the ridge, his German binoculars still in his hands, and his hands were shaking but not with the cold . . .

Han Lu Chen spoke. "They would do it."

The Russian officer, Prokopiev, warmed his hands over the heater/cooker. Annie stirred warm water into a packet of food, the five of them huddled inside the German field shelter. It was dome-shaped, radar-reflective, hermetically sealed against the elements and fitted with a portable climate-control system which ran on pellets of solidified synth fuel, the combination not making them bake with the heat, but keeping the chill low enough that with sweaters on, they could move about comfortably in the confined area with their parkas off. The windchill factor outside the tent was approximately thirty-four degrees below zero Fahrenheit, if the emergency kits from the German Supers were to be believed. And, if anything, Michael Rourke thought they might be registering on the conservative side.

Prokopiev finally spoke. "I cannot believe they would do this. I have spoken with the Comrade Colonel. He wants the nuclear weapons only so that he may threaten to use them and thus end the warfare, not to end the earth."

"Maybe," Annie said matter-of-factly. "It's hard to imagine he wouldn't use them if he had to."

"But—"

She handed the food packet to Prokopiev and looked at him as he took it from her. "Grow up, Vassily, for God's sake! Maybe he isn't your damned hero marshal, but he's no saint either! Antonovitch didn't survive as one of Karamatsov's chief staff officers by being a goodie-goodie, for Christ's sake!"

"She's right, Vassily." Michael nodded, Maria handing him a food packet she'd made for him. He was quite capable of adding hot water to dried food and had been doing it for five centuries, really, the German food in taste not unlike the Mountain House products his father had so favored, identical in preparation. But Maria and Annie, or perhaps Maria because of Annie, liked to busy themselves with the domestic chores of camp, or perhaps only felt they were supposed to. He thought for a moment about Madison, his wife of so little time. She had been at her happiest when caring for him. He closed his eyes, could still see her blond hair and how it caught the light—

Han Lu Chen was talking and Michael Rourke opened his eyes. "These are desperate, war-mongering people, their religion built on violence, their culture stifled, primitive, and perhaps their understanding of the true nature of the weapons which they possess so limited they cannot imagine the destruction of which these weapons are capable. Perhaps they have already begun some irreversible process."

"Madmen," Prokopiev said, barely audible.

"Yes," Maria interjected. "Like the madmen who pushed the first button and began the war that nearly destroyed all life on this planet five centuries ago?"

Prokopiev put his utensil in the food packet and looked at all of them in turn. "The suggestion is that we somehow seek to foil any plans for detonation the Chinese may have?"

"Chinese of the Second City," Han hissed. "My people long ago mastered nuclear power in all respects and would never consider such a barbarous act."

"There's Paul to consider. Once he's found Dad and Natalia," Michael said slowly, "they may need medical help, God knows. And inside that city is no place for a woman. Prokopiev and I have been there. So has Han. If the two of you—" And he looked at Annie and Maria. "If you guys could—"

"You mean if we helpless women were suddenly to become so capable? Bullshit!"

73

"Listen, Annie, huh? If you and Maria go to the rendezvous with Paul and Otto, then get outa here, maybe—" He really didn't know what "maybe" might be. But he was certain he would not allow his sister and/or the woman he was in love with to enter the Second City. He wasn't enthusiastic about allowing himself to do it either. His head still ached from the last time.

"There is confusion everywhere," Prokopiev said. "If you would allow me to contact my own forces, I could run the raid myself and none of you need risk your lives. It would—"

"Vassily," Michael began, "if your people had the nuclear weapons they possess in the Second City, I wouldn't exactly rest easy. And it's not a matter of possession. It's a matter of second guessing just how desperate they are in there, or how stupid, and just what they'll do with their backs to the wall. What was your intelligence assessment of their technological capabilities? Do you think they have the technical expertise to make something go off?"

"We had no way of knowing," Prokopiev said, lowering his head, his face red-tinged by the glow of the heater, his eyes closed.

"And you attacked the Second City?" Annie said incredulously.

"All military operations, Mrs. Rubenstein," Prokopiev announced, raising his head, looking at her, "incorporate a certain amount of calculated risk."

"Incalculable risk!" Annie told him. "You guys are nuts!"

Maria, kneeling beside Michael now, said softly, "Considerable variations of computer models were made concerning the technological abilities of potential survivors of what the Americans refer to as 'the Great Conflagration'—"

"The Dragon Wind," Han Lu Chen nodded.

"Yes," Maria went on. "One of the models I found particularly intriguing, however unlikely, seems to fit in here, and because of that more than anything anyone has said, I am

74

frightened. The computer model dealt with the concept of the medium of destruction in effect metamorphosing, becoming an object of worship since it had, in effect, spared those who survived to worship it. The logic is primitive but valid. And if such a society were to exist—which seems to be the case of the Second City—the model was extended to incorporate the possibility—statistically closer to probability—that some of the mechanics at least of operating such weapons of destruction might indeed become incorporated among the trappings of such a religion, as part of holy ritual, as it were. In theory, at least," Maria Leuden continued, sounding very much the Fraulein Doctor, her gray-green eyes sparkling behind the lenses of her wire-rimmed glasses, "such ritual could be graduated, much as was conventional religion, such as was Christianity or Muhammadanism. The Christians, for example, had certain high holy days, such as Christmas and Easter. The Moslems had their feast of Ramadan. There are countless examples. The Jews, certainly, with their various celebrations commemorating events from their history. If the worshippers of the Second City perceive themselves facing some ultimate crisis, as logic would dictate even the most ardent among them must, then those most ardent among them would seek consolation in their religion, perhaps some special ceremony. Such a special ceremony," Maria concluded, her normally soft alto lowering, "could well include the ritual necessary to arm or detonate a warhead. Sort of calling on the ultimate power of their god, who of course spared them once and, if their propitiations are heeded, would spare them again while at the same time vanquishing their enemies." Her hands suddenly clasped Michael's left bicep, very tightly.

No one spoke.

Michael Rourke just stared at the palms of his hands, listening to everyone breathing, to the soft hiss of the heater/cooker, the muted howl of the wind outside, to the slapping sounds as a gust of wind struck at the shelter broadside. "We go inside if we can get there. There isn't any choice." And, inside himself, he knew he'd be a fool if he didn't take Maria Leuden with him. What was in her mind might be their only chance for success. Survival beyond that was something his own logic dictated he shouldn't waste the effort to consider.

# Chapter Fourteen

Paul Rubenstein and Otto Hammerschmidt prepared to cross the river, Hammerschmidt saying, "Idle speculation, I know, my friend, but if only I had the facility to call up our combat engineers. We would have a bridge across which a tank could be taken and it would be erected in under ten minutes."

"The Russians had machines like that five centuries ago."

"I studied them. German is better." Hammerschmidt smiled wolfishly. Paul Rubenstein just shook his head. There was no bridge-laying equipment, just the rappeling gear from the emergency equipment aboard the Specials. And he smiled at the thought of the person at whose insistence each item of emergency equipment had been included. John Rourke, his friend, his father-in-law, in the most real sense of the word his mentor, had, once again, planned ahead.

With the ropes there was a grappling hook which fired from a disposable launcher, the launcher disposable because it was not repackable in the field, the rope under mechanical compression. The ropes were flat, made of something which reminded Rubenstein of the Kevlar material John had once shown him in a bullet-resistant vest. The launchers were designed to fire upward, so he assumed they would fire outward as well. But, before Otto Hammerschmidt had mentioned it, Paul had realized it was a matter of trajectory, holding high enough that the spring-loaded grappling hooks would deploy over the object to which they hoped for attachment rather than level with or below it.

They had traveled down along the river's course for more than an hour, scouting a potential crossing, at last settling on a gap perhaps twenty-five yards across. But it was the depth that bothered him. The gorge through which the river cut so violently was at least seventy-five feet below them, and white-water rapids made the water glow eerily despite the otherwise poor visibility of the snowstorm.

Since it was impossible to get the Specials across, they had argued over it, then eventualy flipped a German coin for it. Paul Rubenstein had won. He would cross, explore the opposite bank on foot, Hammerschmidt waiting with the Specials.

"Are you ready, Paul?"

Rubenstein brushed snowflakes from his eyelashes and nodded. Before he had taken the Sleep he'd worn glasses, and in snow or rain they naturally became wet and were difficult to see through. But without them the snow or rain assaulted the eyes directly. He reflected that one couldn't win.

"I'm ready," he lied, because he was at once impatient to be gone but reluctant to crawl across the rope spanning the gorge when it would be attached on the opposite side only by an almost randomly positioned grappling hook.

Hammerschmidt put the launcher to his right shoulder. "A pity it doesn't have sights," the German commando captain remarked.

"A real pity, yes," Rubenstein agreed, wiping more snow from his eyes.

"Then here it is." And as if punctuating his words, the launcher fired with a pneumatic hiss so flat-sounding that it reminded Paul Rubenstein of someone passing gas.

His eyes tracked the roughly conical shape as it shot over the gorge, the flat rope uncoiling in its wake like a snake run over by a truck on some country road five centuries ago. He realized absently that he was wondering if somewhere on earth snakes survived. But before he decided anything concerning that, the conical shape of the grappling hook device disappeared into a swirl of snow. Hammerschmidt fell to tugging at the rope, Rubenstein helping, the rope suddenly going taut.

They both threw their weight on the rope, trying to pull it free lest it work itself free. The rope was taut as a flat piece of metal.

Together, they tied it off into the rocks near them, then further secured it to a tree, discarding the launcher, Hammerschmidt saying, "I'll bury the launcher in the snow once you are across."

"Hopefully that's all you'll bury. Gimme a hand." Together, they manipulated one of the Specials into position beneath the stretched taut rope, Paul Rubenstein tightening the sling of his Schmeisser submachine gun, tightening the strap of the musette bag in which he carried its spare magazines. He checked the safety strap of the tanker-style holster in which his battered Browning High Power was carried. These two firearms and his Gerber MK II knife were all he would take, the bulk of his arctic gear and the need to move fast and potentially far on foot defining his practical limits.

"Are you certain that you will not change your mind, Paul? I could rope over a rifle and a small pack and—"

"No—gotta travel light. Gimme a leg up." He mounted the saddle of the Special, then grabbed the rope with his gloved hands, Hammerschmidt taking his feet, helping him as he swung them up and over the rope. The rope was already crusting with ice.

"Any famous last words?"

"Yeah, but I'm too polite to say them." Rubenstein made himself laugh. And he started moving out, feet first, hand-over-hand, Hammerschmidt helping him the last three yards or so until he reached the edge; then he was out, over the gorge, the wind shrieking like a tortured soul, lashing at his body, at the rope, the flat rope vibrating with it. "I think I can, I think I can," he murmured, already short of breath, moving steadily, not daring to stop.

Below—he cursed his stupidity for looking down—white water crashed over the rocks and flickered up toward him with beckoning fingers. He shook his head, kept moving, gauging it now that he was at the approximate center of the gorge, at the point of no return where it no longer made sense to even attempt to turn back. But he could not in any event. He kept moving, wishing suddenly he still smoked, thinking about Annie—he loved her and she loved him, and if none of the other things that had happened to him since meeting John Rourke aboard that flight into Atlanta that was diverted to New Mexico on the very Night of the War could be considered miraculous, then their love could. She was so exquisitely pretty, brilliant, headstrong, gentle, loving—everything he had ever wanted in life was part of her. Paul Rubenstein kept moving.

Someday, they'd have a child—more than one. He found himself smiling—John a grandfather.

Paul looked down again, his fingers stiffening, his legs and forearms cramping, his shoulders aching. He remembered—he actually remembered nothing of it beyond what he was told after he recovered—John Rourke edging across just such a precarious rope to rescue him from a flaming helicopter in the aftermath of Karamatsov's attack on the landing Eden Project shuttle crafts. The pain was something John had felt. John hadn't given up. Paul kept going, his fingers barely able to close, the cold numbing him too now, the wind gusting, tearing at him. His hood blew down and his ears and face suddenly tingled with the cold.

He kept moving. And then the rope vibrated more strongly than it had before and he didn't move. Upside down, he looked back, barely able to see Hammerschmidt by the very edge, Hammerschmidt gesticulating wildly, evidently shouting but his words lost on the wind. But the understanding was there. Hammerschmidt evidently thought the grappling hook was working loose.

Paul Rubenstein looked ahead, the rope vibrating strongly

again, rocks of immense size and jagged shape on the opposite wall of the gorge. He could cut the rope, swing toward the opposite wall of the gorge, hope to cling to something.

The rope lurched and Paul Rubenstein felt a sudden sick feeling in the pit of his stomach, an instant of total weightlessness, then a shock to his arms and legs and back.

The rope swayed maddeningly.

He realized the grappling hook's position had shifted.

Cut the rope and swing toward the wall?

And what if he struck against the rocks so hard that he died? Annie a widow in a world like this? And John. And Natalia. "No!" Paul Rubenstein shouted into the wind. He started moving again, but the ice on the rope now that it swayed was making him lose traction, and for each inch he moved forward, he slipped an inch downward, his relative position unchanged.

Rubenstein licked his lips. His cheeks and ears were numb with the cold. With his right hand, he reached out, as far ahead of his torso as he could. And then he swung his left leg from the rope, the rope vibrating maddeningly. He hung there, his left knee carrying much of his weight, both fists clenched to the ice-slicked synthetic rope.

With difficulty—nothing he knew compared to what lay ahead—he cleared his left leg of the rope, hanging there for a frightening instant by his hands alone, gusts of wind ripping at him, snow and spicules of ice pelting his exposed flesh.

He snarled at the wind, as if somehow it were a mortal enemy, at the night, at the snow, at the rocks and the raging white water below him, then pulled. He'd never been the world's greatest athlete, having discovered muscles in his adulthood he'd never known he had as a child, but he swung his right elbow over the rope, the rope, despite its flatness, gouging through his parka and into his flesh and musculature, his arm tingling with the pain.

He threw himself up and forward, hurtling his left leg over the rope, for an instant what little balance he had gone as he slipped forward, his right arm moving quickly, his gloved fist closing over the rope. He hung there, breathing, glad for the opportunity.

His right leg—he swung it upward.

He was now faced in the opposite direction, could use his feet for leverage against the rope, its very flatness now his enemy. He hung there, but only for another moment, the numbness of exhaustion which was overtaking him an enemy still worse. He started moving again, wedging the rope between the outer edges of his crisscrossed feet, pushing with his feet as he pulled upward and forward with his hands.

He was moving.

He thought of Annie. Was she warm?

John and Natalia. They had to be alive. He could see Hammerschmidt faintly, waving to him. Why? Encouraging him onward, cheering his survival?

Paul Rubenstein kept going.

And then, as he narrowed the gap to the far side of the gorge to under ten yards, he heard a rifle shot, coming from Hammerschmidt's side. Had the German commando gone mad? "Otto!" A bullet whined off the rocks ahead of him, only faintly audible under the keening of the wind.

He kept moving.

As Paul Rubenstein looked up—more gunshots, bursts of rifle fire now—he saw what Hammerschmidt was shooting at.

He saw why the rope had slipped, why it vibrated again even now.

The Chinese of the Second City had the most peculiar ideas of animal husbandry, he thought absently. Not only had they released wolves into the environment.

But they had released at least one bear.

# Chapter Fifteen

John Rourke's eyes opened. "Shots—" He had fallen asleep, he realized only now.

Shots—but not a helicopter's mini-guns. Automatic rifle shots, some distance away but not too terribly far, because outside, as his senses came fully alert, he realized that the wind howled, in its ferocity even greater than before. The log—he pushed it into the fire, a shower of sparks rising, but the dampening effect of the snow on their shelter was enough that there was no concern for fire. It wasn't so warm within the shelter that he would have felt comfortable removing his shirt, but it wasn't so cold that he felt uncomfortable without his sweater.

John Rourke sat up, his right hand automatically closed on the butt of one of the little Detonics .45s, his left hand resting on Natalia's blanketed right leg. After feeding her, he had gone over the rock ledge into the deep drifts there by the height of the gorge and washed her clothing after she had dirtied herself and her garments, then brought the things back, suspended them over the fire to dry.

Natalia was sleeping still, and he realized she was sleeping too much and that he was only keeping her body alive while her mind kept slipping farther away.

More shots.

He was standing.

Rourke reached for the shoulder harness for the twin

stainless Detonics and shrugged into it, holstering one gun, then the second. The Scoremasters. He grabbed them, thrust them into his belt.

He looked at Natalia.

He grabbed his gunbelt . . .

Paul Rubenstein hung onto the shuddering rope with his left hand and both knees and feet, biting off the other glove from his right hand, his helmet slung from his musette bag, slamming into his abdomen as he twisted round, his right hand moving under his coat, grasping for the butt of the Browning.

The creature was not so large as bears he'd seen in zoos or stuffed in museums, not a Kodiak or a polar bear, just a black bear of huge proportions and bulk, a white airfoil-shaped mask of fur beneath his eyes and over his mouth, giving the effect of some hideously inane smile.

Paul thumbed back the hammer. The sub-machinegun would have been better, but there was no way to release the sling one-handed without risking dropping it into the river below.

More automatic weapons fire from Otto Hammerschmidt's side of the gorge.

"Get outa here!" Rubenstein shouted as the animal grabbed at the rope with one huge paw, then another. It stood nearly upright, stared at him, then bent over the rope, pulling at it, the rope slipping again, Rubenstein nearly losing his pistol, the grappling hook visible now, barely wedged in the rocks near the animal's feet.

Paul Rubenstein fired a double tap, then again and again, the bear howling with rage, stepping back, then reaching downward to swat at the rope once again.

Rubenstein fired again, the grappling hook starting to dislodge . . .

*        *        *

John Rourke ran, the pistol shots he'd just heard convincing him that it was something other than Russians or fleeing Second City Chinese. The 629 in his right fist, he clambered up into the natural rock wall which separated the wooded area in which he had made camp from the river, the shots coming from a considerable distance upriver along the course of the gorge, his hearing placing the origin of the rifle shots and the pistol shots some distance apart. A gunbattle between two men?

He kept running, along the river's edge now, the snow falling more heavily, movement more difficult than it had been before. Snowshoes would be mandatory by morning. He kept running, more pistol shots, something oddly but unconsciously familiar about them. More assault rifle fire, the sound not right for an M-16, more like the German weapons— "Hammerschmidt"—Rourke quickened his pace, pulling his parka hood up against the numbing cold, running.

If help were coming, then Natalia—

He kept running . . .


The Browning High Power's slide locked open, the pistol empty, the bear howling with rage, swatting at the grappling hook as if somehow the hook itself were the source of the pain the animal had to be feeling from the multiple hits it had sustained without going down.

Paul Rubenstein's cold-numbed right thumb worked the battered Browning's slide release downward, the slide skating forward. There was no chance to reload, and no time either. As quickly as he could, he shoved the 9mm back into the tanker holster, closing the safety strap against loss, taking his outer glove from his teeth, working his hand into it, then starting along the rope again.

More assault rifle fire from Hammerschmidt's side of the gorge, the bear—as he neared it, it seemed larger—hammering so mightily at the grappling hook that the flat Kevlar-like rope was swaying now like some sort of hammock in a breeze.

Seven yards now, five. The bear seemed to be losing interest in the grappling hook, taking interest in him.

Paul Rubenstein thought of the Gerber knife, a stout blade but slim defense against a creature this size.

His only defense. There would be no time for the subgun and no time to reload the High Power. No time to run either.

The grappling hook slipped again and he almost lost his handholds, the rope bellying out and down, his body slamming against the rocks, skidding.

He wedged his right foot and stopped himself, embracing the firmness of the rocks with his body, breathing.

He looked up. There was a natural path, and the bear was starting down along it, growling more fiercely than before.

Rubenstein tried remembering everything he could about bears. Generally poor eyesight. Not all bears hibernated, although in extreme temperatures like these— But what was an extreme temperature for a bear?

He had never been a hunter, had shot men before he'd ever shot game. He tried to gauge its weight—at least five hundred pounds. If a five hundred pound angry man were coming at him, immune to pain, interested only in ripping him to shreds, what would he do? He laughed despite it all. The likely answer to his self-questioning was obvious: he would most likely die. With the foothold, he was able to reach for the High Power, buttoning out the magazine into his left hand as the hand still held the rope, but unable to twist himself around sufficiently to get at the musette bag.

In his pockets. He searched his outside pockets, finding a spare thirteen-round magazine, bracing the magazine between his heaving chest and the magazine well, pushing it up and home. The slide was closed. "Damn!" He shagged the pistol against his pants, having seen John Rourke doing that once— "Sight snubbing is what they used to call it, Paul. It's something to practice occasionally in the event you need to work the slide of your pistol and have only one hand operable enough to do it. I used to teach the technique to women who insisted on keeping to a pistol they weren't physically strong enough to operate. Only in that case, I'd have them brace the rear sight against a table edge or some other hard object. Not too good for the rear sight and only useful in a home defense context and not very sure. But anything in a pinch if you have to."

Paul Rubenstein stabbed the rear sight of the Browning into his thigh and rammed the pistol downward, the slide coming back, then, as he released, snapping forward.

The bear was three yards above him on the rocky path that would take the creature into range with its long front limbs, into range to rip his body to shreds with its enormous claws—a bear's claws had to be enormous. He realized his hand was shaking as he took aim with the High Power.

From above him, Paul Rubenstein heard a familiar voice. "Is it good to see you, Paul!"

He looked toward the sound, for an instant saw John Rourke bending over the edge of the precipice, then in John's hands he saw the .44 Magnum revolver (John had begun carrying the 629 after the accident involving his Colt Python). And then there was an earsplitting crack, the rocks ringing with it and the sound, despite the wind, echoing and re-echoing with it, the creature's forehead seeming to burst, exploding in a cloud of pink and red and gray. And the bear just swayed there for what seemed like forever, clawing toward the snow-obscured sky, then tumbling forward suddenly. And suddenly, Paul Rubenstein felt shame and rage that this creature whose species had survived so much had had to die.

He looked up into the face of John Rourke. John Rourke spoke to him over the keening of the wind. "I know what you're thinking; I didn't want to kill it, but there wasn't any choice. I need your help." And John Rourke began clambering down the path the bear had followed, holstering his revolver, still talking. "Does your helmet radio work? Can you reach the base radio?"

"We didn't want to use it. The Russians could pick it up.

And I'm out of range now, but we have a rendezvous. How's Natalia?" He was almost afraid to speak her name. Where was she?

"Very sick," his friend told him as he reached out from the path and Paul, his pistol holstered, reached back and their hands clasped. "Thank God you came."

# Chapter Sixteen

There was substantial likelihood that the gunfire would draw enemy personnel, either Russian or from the scattered forces of the Second City which had borne the brunt of the initial phases of the Soviet attack.

Paul Rubenstein walked beside John Rourke, although his muscles screamed at him to rest. John had simply said, "We'll have to hurry—there isn't much time."

Using his helmet radio, Paul had relayed to Otto Hammerschmidt on the other side of the gorge that John Rourke was well but that Natalia was somehow injured and they were going now to aid her and that he—Hammerschmidt—should stand by and watch for possible interdiction by enemy forces.

It was bitter cold, but with the hood of his parka restored, at least his ears and cheeks were beginning to thaw. He noticed that the left sleeve of John's parka was torn and carefully resewn, and noticed as well bloodstains on John's right sleeve. "What happened?" he said over the howling of the wind.

"Everything that could possibly go wrong did—almost. We were pursued by Second City Chinese forces and there were Soviet gunships on us as well. I did the only thing I could." John Rourke stopped dead in his tracks and looked at him very earnestly.

"What happened?" Paul asked, not wanting to know.

"Natalia was already behaving strangely," John Rourke

resumed, resuming walking as well. "We went over the side into the gorge. We lost the Special, got soaked to the skin. All she was doing was repeating my name, over and over again—"

"Han said something about—"

"She's completely withdrawn into herself. I'm no psychiatrist, but I think she's suffering from manic depression."

"She snapped—"

John Rourke wheeled toward him and for a split second Paul Rubenstein thought that his friend might strike him, the energy in John Rourke's eyes then like something he had never seen before. "Yes—I think so. Come on."

They clambered over a rock ledge and down, the snow somehow less deep as they neared the treeline, then veered left. Ahead, in the distance, he saw the dull glow of a fire. "I had to risk a fire. She was freezing again—"

"Did, ahh—"

"What?"

"Did she say anything else at all?"

"No. In the last few hours she may have become incontinent. It was almost impossible to feed her."

"Then you salvaged some food—"

John Rourke smiled. "The wolves that were said to have been loosed by the Second City people—they're feral dogs." And John Rourke patted at the torn sleeve of his parka. "But well-prepared, they provided adequate nourishment with the pine bark paste."

"Yuck!"

"That too." Rourke smiled.

They were nearing the fire, a lean-to of sorts constructed out of snow-laden pine boughs partially covering the fire as well.

As they stopped before it, John Rourke grabbed his arm. "Whatever, I'm responsible for this. And we have to get her to help. Perhaps the Germans, or at Mid-Wake. I don't know." He released Paul Rubenstein's arm and they entered the shelter, the warmth comparatively stifling to him with the sudden absence of the wind. Something smelled very good and his eyes traveled to the fire which was built in two segments, one evidently for cooking and more controlled, the other for warmth. On a line made from some sort of vine, a woman's undergarment—a teddy?—was draped, as well as Natalia's customary black jumpsuit. He looked at John Rourke, then back to the fire. Over the cooking portion of the fire was a kettle that appeared to be made of paper-thin bark, food simmering in it—the dogmeat? His eyes passed from the fire and the disgusting-sounding but appealing-smelling meal to the shape in the far corner.

Huddled beneath a parka and an emergency blanket was Natalia Anastasia Tiemerovna, her normally pale complexion paler still, her eyelids fluttering, lips parched-looking, pale and drawn, moving as though reciting some inaudible litany.

John went to her, and as he moved her slightly, kneeling beside her now, part of the coverings fell away and Paul could see that she wore John's gray woolen sweater. And there was a smell of human waste. John Rourke looked up from his knees beside her and Paul Rubenstein looked into his friend's eyes.

"Paul—" Tears filled John Rourke's eyes . . .

He supposed he would have felt more awkward if he were not a married man, but it hadn't helped him that much. And he was stunned by her physical beauty as he helped John Rourke dress her. She wasn't more beautiful than Annie, and he told himself that indeed Annie was the most beautiful woman in the world. But each muscle, each limb— In her nakedness, Natalia Anastasia Tiemerovna reminded him of the masterwork of some great sculptor. And, a man of religious feeling, he thought that perhaps in fact she was.

John had bathed her with warm water from the fire and as Rubenstein now began to put out the fire, John buried the emergency blanket. It was unclaimable. The sweater suffered the same fate.

Natalia kept repeating "John . . . John . . . John . . ." And Paul Rubenstein wept as well . . .


Annie Rourke Rubenstein could not sleep. She was the

logical one to be left behind and she knew that and she respected logic, but she hated its result. Michael, to do what needed to be done; Maria, because of her understanding of archeology and anthropology and her greater familiarity with computer technology; Han Lu Chen because of his Chinese appearance, knowledge of the language and greater knowledge of the Chinese Second City. And she was left to travel alone to the rendezvous.

She closed her eyes tightly as she had when she was a little girl and had been told that it was bedtime, and she couldn't sleep. And she couldn't sleep now.

It was almost time to take the Special they'd left her and go on toward the rendezvous. And she was cold, despite the climate-controlled small tent in which she huddled.

Things to do.

Dismantle the tent.

Make it to the rendezvous.

Things to do.

She sat up and suddenly felt Natalia's pain deep inside her, and there was confusion such as she had never known. And despair . . .


Sarah Rourke hugged the thermal blanket closer around her, by the light of the lanterns watching the grim faces of Colonel Wolfgang Mann and his officers as they pored over the maps she had spent the better part of the day drawing, her right thumb aching.

A third of the First Chinese City was occupied by the Soviet invaders, including the government buildings. And, to make matters worse, while Colonel Mann's forces had been airborne, dealing heavy blows to the Soviet gunships, Soviet ground forces had attacked the only marginally defended basecamp, killed the men stationed there and kidnapped the Chinese chairman and his party.

The government of the First City was in the hands of the

Soviets, but Chinese forces were resisting valiantly.

Colonel Mann had told her simply, "You may not be through yet with your duties, Frau Rourke, if I may be so presumptuous; I suggest that you rest."

And, for the baby's sake, she had rested, thankful that conscious dreaming was something she no longer experienced. The terror of being awake was enough.

And Colonel Mann had sent one of his officers to awaken her with a message: "You are needed, Frau Rourke; please come at once." His handwriting looked like calligraphy and was very beautiful. She had come.

And at last he turned away from the map table and looked across the tent toward her. "I have, Frau Rourke, spent considerable time in attempting to find a suitable alternative; and I have found no alternative nearly as laden with hope for success as that you should accompany us into the city. Your intimacy with the government complex is beyond that which can be hoped to be achieved from any map. If you say no, I will fully understand."

"Would your wife say no? Did she when my husband and I and the others helped your city?"

And by the lantern light, she saw a smile raise the corners of his mouth. He clicked his heels as he bowed quickly to her, then said, "Gentlemen—" His officers saluted her and she felt herself beginning to blush . . .


Kurinami studied the green lights of the control console, calling to his doorgunner without using the radio. "Corporal?"

"All is in order, Herr Lieutenant."

"Headset on, then—good luck."

"The same to you, Herr Lieutenant."

Kurinami adjusted his headset, then spoke. "This is Retribution Leader to Squadron—acknowledge this radio test and stand by. Begin."

One by one, the pilots of his few gunships responded in

sequence; then Kurinami spoke again. "This is Retribution Leader. We will pass over the foothills and attack the Soviet base from the west as planned. Maintain radio silence except in an emergency until engagement. Retribution Leader out." And he clicked off. They were not, of course, planning to pass over the foothills and attack from the west. If the Soviet gunships refueling and re-arming in the narrow valley to the north did not have the German radio frequencies monitored, he missed his guess. And he would be dead.

He gave a last-minute check to his instruments and got the fast-handling German gunship airborne, light snow still falling but visibility satisfactory.

There was a funnel-shaped canyon which was exceedingly narrow, and it was guarded on both sides by heavy machine guns, as his ground reconnaissance had confirmed before dark. But only two guns on each side. And one missile battery backing up the double machine-gun teams on each side. It was obvious why, although it provided direct access into the Soviet staging area: the canyon was considered too narrow and that, added to the natural updrafts such geographic features were noted for, made attempting a raid through the canyon tantamount to suicide. Which, of course, made it the only logical approach.

Akiro Kurinami changed pitches and slipped the machine northward and down, terrain following the dried riverbed which had, centuries before, cut the canyon from granite.

He looked to right and left, his squadron beginning to take up the attack formation, a single column, following his lead.

He glanced at his wristwatch. In five minutes, the canyon.

# Chapter Seventeen

In the distance, muted but unmistakably distinct from the howling of the wind and the creaking of the pines, John Thomas Rourke heard the throbbing of rotors. The Soviet helicopter gunships consumed fuel at a higher rate when they operated in the silenced mode, and their presence in this area near the Second Chinese City was certainly no secret. Tactically, it was obvious they would not waste the fuel needed for silent operation.

He ran, Natalia cradled in his arms like an exhausted and terribly sick child, Paul Rubenstein beside him, Paul evidently hearing the Soviet gunships as well, the bolt of his German MP-40 submachine gun snapping open.

"John!"

"Signal Hammerschmidt to get your Specials out of sight. They won't spot that rope across the gorge from the air. Pray they don't spot the shelter I built." Natalia was just as vulnerable as a child, just as helpless, just as needing of protection. The visibility was so poor now with the increasing snowfall that, when the wind gusted and snow whirled up in its wake, Paul was lost from sight for a few seconds at a time. Rourke didn't envy the Soviet pilots. Natalia kept moving her lips, dry and parched to the touch of his hand, reciting her now barely audible mantra, his name.

"Rest now—I'm here," he told her, knowing inside himself that she didn't hear him and that telling her anything was merely masturbating his conscience. She seemed so fragile to him, and he had never realized before how really fragile she had always been. From childhood, she had possessed precious little of any true identity; and, in her work for Soviet intelligence as a major in the KGB, so much of her day-to-day life had demanded subordinating real identity to the currently operational lie.

He stopped as he heard the bolt slamming back on Paul Rubenstein's submachine gun.

"This way—into the trees." Paul only nodded, his lips moving like Natalia's, but relaying instructions to Otto Hammerschmidt, Rourke knew. Rourke's own helmet and Natalia's clanked against Paul's side, strung together there, Rourke's hands and arms filled. "Here!" And Rourke turned into the tree cover, finding the densest overhead he could, then flattening himself against one of the trunks, Paul doing the same just a few feet away. Rourke held Natalia's head close against his chest.

The whirring of the rotor blades was louder now and the pattern of snowfall changed, driven straight downward, then twisting cyclonically. At least one of the machines was dead overhead.

Rourke clutched Natalia tightly to him, his right fist clenching on the butt of one of the Scoremasters, getting it awkwardly from his trouser band, the hammer down, his thumb poised over it.

He watched Paul Rubenstein's face. The younger man nodded.

The storm of snow around them increased in violence. The helicopter was dropping to a lower altitude.

Paul raised the muzzle of the submachine gun and for a moment John Rourke thought he was going to open fire, but his faith in Paul's competence and cool-headedness made him dismiss such thoughts.

Paul only waited.

John Rourke waited, Natalia murmuring agitatedly.

He forced his mind away from this. Once the choppers had gone, he and Paul and Natalia could continue on toward the gorge—himself, Paul, Natalia, just as it had been in the days between the Night of the War and the Great Conflagration, but now a grotesque parody.

Rourke's eyes followed the rising and falling of her chest, the fluttering of her eyelids.

The helicopter still hovered low above them.

How many gunships?

He forced his mind away from them again. Once at the gorge, some way or another they would rope Natalia across, then cross the gorge themselves, then use the two Specials to reach the rendezvous site. Then risk the radio to signal for extraction. But what if—

The answer to his question came from above: less than a dozen yards from their position, first one, then a second, then a third and fourth rope tumbled from the sky. Down the first rope a man rappeled with marvelous fluidity, his clothes the black battle uniform of the KGB Elite Corps, a Soviet assault rifle in his right fist.

John Rourke dropped to his knees in the snow, putting Natalia down. There was no chance to run, only fight, and perhaps providence had a hand in that.

As Rourke looked up, a second man was dropping, Paul shouting, "Look out!" The submachine gun roared, the second Elite corpsman blown from his rope into the snow. John Rourke stabbed the Detonics pistol in his right hand toward the first man as the assault rifle the Russian held opened up, stitching across the tree trunks, snow falling in great globs as the trees were impacted, Rourke thumbing the hammer to full stand, his gloved right first finger touching the trigger, the gleaming full-sized .45 moving gently against his hand, the Elite corpsman's chin suddenly crumbling, the body rocking back as the assault rifle kept firing, but firing skyward.

John Rourke ran now, Paul beside him. "Paul—stay near her!"

"I will—what—"

But John Rourke's right hand was already safing the Scoremaster, ramming it into his trouser band, his left hand reaching out for the rappeling rope, the Elite corpsman crawling across the snow, a bloodtrail in his wake, a pistol in his hand. Rourke had the rope and swung up and outward, the toe of his right boot impacting the middle of the face. The Elite corpsman's head snapped back.

Rourke's right fist caught the rope, his legs around it, his hands moving, his feet pushing. He'd always been physically strong, enjoyed exercise and good health, been a good athlete as a young man—but he had never enjoyed climbing a free rope. Hand over hand now, up, toward the chopper.

A third Elite corpsman was rappeling down, a look of bewilderment in his eyes, a burst of sub-machinegun fire from the ground, his body jackknifing, then spiraling downward. Rourke kept climbing.

The fourth KGB man on the fourth rope. He slowed his descent, stopped, John Rourke throwing his body weight, catching the Elite corpsman full in the face with the sole of his boot, the man screaming as he lost his handhold, a sickeningly audible crack as the body bowed unnaturally back and death filled the eyes, the back broken.

His rope still swinging, John Rourke kept climbing, his arms numbing, hands aching, but only a few feet to go.

Above him, hanging out of the open fuselage door, an Elite corpsman leveled an assault rifle.

Rourke's right hand went to the Scoremaster in his belt, already cocked and locked, submachine gun fire coming toward the man in the door from Paul on the ground, the man tucking back, but Paul only buying time. To hit the man, Rourke knew, Paul could only have shot through and not around him. But it bought a second, Rourke stabbing the Scoremaster upward. The Elite corpsman was in the doorway again, firing. John Rourke fired, then again and again and again and again and again, the Elite corpsman's body twisting, then tumbling forward, impacting Rourke's own body as he fell past, Rourke's left shoulder feeling on fire as he sagged away and hung for a moment suspended only from his left hand. The Scoremaster was still in his right hand. It was let go of it or die. He let it go, shouting, "Look out, Paul!"

Rourke's right hand slapped upward, grasping for the rope, and as his right hand caught it, the helicopter began moving, violently upward and left, Rourke's legs impacting the upper branches of a pine, part of his left snowpants leg torn away, a shower of snow covering him.

A second chopper and a third, flanking the machine to which John Rourke clung, were closing fast, mini-guns opening up, great tongues of yellow flame etched across the swirling gray that washed over the night's blackness. Rourke curled his right leg around the rope, but still the strain on his hands and arms and shoulders consumed him, his teeth clenched against the pain.

The helicopter banked sharply and slipped closer to the treetops now; Rourke's legs and torso slammed into another of the pines, then dragged through it, more of his arctic gear shredding under the impact, branches hammering at his face, tearing the hood from his head. Mini-gun fire again, so close his ears rang with it, the treetop over which he was dragged disintegrating under its impact, a shower of pine needles and snow washing over his face. Rourke averted his eyes, wrenching his right arm upward along the rope, his right fist bunching around it, his feet slamming into more of the high branches, more of his snowpants torn away.

Rourke's left fist moved along the rope, then his right again and his left.

Mini-gun fire, so close that he felt some of the rounds cutting the air near his face, his teeth clenching, his fists balling tighter to the rope.

His right fist moved, then his left, then his right and his left again, the rope biting into his thighs, his fingers stiffening.

The helicopter from which he swung was going for

elevation, the G-forces against him pushing him down, his hands fighting to keep their hold. And then the gunship dove. Rourke's face was twisted against the pressure of wind and gravity, but he felt the corners of his mouth rising into a smile; the Soviet pilot's cleverness would be his undoing. As the chopper dove straight for the treetops, the restraining pressures of the climb were reversed and Rourke could move more easily along the rope now, at times the rope more vertical than diagonal in relation to the gunship.

He had nearly reached the top.

And suddenly the machine veered upward and left, the rope whiplashing forward and right, John Rourke's body with it, the motion so violent his arms were nearly wrenched from their sockets. No longer could he climb. He could only hold on. The machine dove again, the tail of the rappeling rope snagging in the treetops over which the gunship passed, the rope suddenly going taut, vibrating, Rourke's body pulsing with it, then the rope springing, a massive segment of the treetop tearing away from the main trunk, slamming toward him.

Rourke buried his face against his shoulder, the impact coming, lacerating his back and shoulders and legs. His legs lost contact with the rope and he clung now by his hands only. He was spinning, spinning, his stomach churning, his vision blurring, the muscles in his back and shoulders and neck feeling as if they were on fire.

The helicopter began to climb, Rourke's fists numbed, fingers stiff, but as it climbed suddenly, the rope was pulled taut beneath it and Rourke's right calf twisted into it and he steadied himself, climbing again, his head reeling, the contents of his stomach rising into his throat.

The machine was ski-fitted, and John Rourke reached up, his left fist getting to the ski, then his left elbow slipping over it.

He breathed, almost vomiting.

He moved his right arm, over the ski, then his right leg, the open fuselage door just above him.

He started to reach for it.

A face appeared in the doorway, a pistol in a black-gloved hand. There was no time for anything else. John Rourke reached up, grabbed for the BDU front and threw his body weight back. As the pistol discharged, a bullet whining off the ski inches from Rourke's right leg, sparks flying from it, Rourke wrenched his body back, the black-BDU-clad Elite corpsman tumbling from the fuselage door and falling, Rourke's eyes automatically following him as he fell. Arms and legs thrashed maddeningly and John Rourke thought he heard a scream.

Rourke's left hand reached up, caught the lip of the fuselage doorway and he pushed himself up, the door suddenly beginning to close, another Elite corpsman—but it wasn't. It was the pilot. The door was wedged against Rourke's left hand, the man's full body weight against it, Rourke screaming with the pain, then shouting, "Damn you—no!" Rourke's right leg was braced on the ski and he pushed, launching his upper body upward, into the opening for the doorway.

Blows rained down on his head and neck, Rourke's right hand groping for any part of his enemy, his left hand still numbed with pain, the fingers possibly broken. As a boot missed his face by inches, Rourke's right fist closed, at the apex of the triangle made by the KGB pilot's legs, scrotum crushing in Rourke's grasp, the pilot screaming hideously.

John Rourke was up, hurtling the pilot against the opposite bulkhead, the pilot's right knee smashing upward, John Rourke twisting left, taking the blow against his left hip, Rourke's right fist hammering upward, impacting bone hard, the pilot's head snapping back.

Rourke's numbed left hammered forward, into the solar plexus, a powerful left crossing John Rourke's jaw, Rourke's head snapping back, his mind momentarily stunned. The Soviet pilot's right fist rammed forward, Rourke twisting away just in time, taking the blow on the side of his neck. Rourke's left backhanded across the bridge of the Soviet pilot's nose, blood spraying against the starboard side of the fuselage. As Rourke's right hammered forward, the helicopter's orientation to the ground suddenly shifted and John Rourke's feet were swept from under him; he sprawled forward along the cargo area, into a metal ammo cannister, his left shoulder taking the impact.

And he suddenly realized what should have been obvious. The Soviet gunship was on auto pilot. And something had gone wrong.

The pilot—a short man but stockily built, barrel-chested— half sprawled, half threw himself toward Rourke. Rourke's body twisting right, his left throwing forward, impacting bone, a scream from the pilot. Rourke was up, falling against the fuselage, almost falling through the open doorway. And then the machine's attitude shifted, the fuselage door starting to slide to violently. Rourke moved his head, the door slamming closed, then as the aircraft shifted again, the door slid back, the roar of the wind again, the fuselage doorway fully open.

The pilot lunged, John Rourke's fists hammering him down, the pilot's head burrowing into Rourke's abdomen, fists flying toward Rourke's own abdomen and crotch.

Rourke bunched both fists together, hammering them down over the back of the pilot's neck; then suddenly Rourke's legs were ripped from under him and the helicopter changed attitude once again.

Rourke fell back, the upper half of his body extended over nothing but air, the Soviet pilot's right, then his left, then his right, hammering at John Rourke's midsection.

Rourke's left—the fingers barely moved—grabbed at the man's face, catching hold of the right ear, ripping, a hideous scream issuing from the pilot's twisted lips.

Rourke released the ear and made a short, hard jab with his left, the pilot's head snapping back.

Rourke edged back, inside, the pilot's knee smashing upward, Rourke's right thigh blocking it from its intended target. Rourke was on his knees, hauling the pilot's head up for a blow; then suddenly the pilot's left fist held a knife. As it flashed forward, John Rourke's right snapped out, catching the man under the left eye.

The pilot's right slammed into Rourke's left temple and Rourke's balance was gone. He sprawled back. The knife thrust down toward him and Rourke's left knee smashed up, the pilot lurching away, the knife stabbing into the fuselage decking. Rourke's left fist crossed the pilot's jaw. The pilot fell away.

Rourke started to his feet, a solid kick to his midsection sending him back. And then the pilot's full body weight was behind the door, the helicopter's attitude changing again, the pilot's body sprawling forward, the door slamming, Rourke's neck in its path. Rourke's right foot kicked outward and upward, into the pilot's groin, Rourke's right hand bracing against the door.

John Rourke looked down once, the gunship skimming over the snowladen treetops, ice spicules pelting Rourke's face in the main rotor's downdraft.

Rourke crossed the pilot's jaw with a left, then another and another and another, the pilot's body sprawling back. Rourke slumped back. The door was slamming closed and he moved his head, a few hairs from the top catching in it, tearing out.

Rourke was up, the pilot up only to his knees, John Rourke's right hammering down, then his left, then his right, Rourke's left knee slamming upward, into the pilot's jaw.

Rourke reached for the arm, dragging him up to his feet, the helicopter shifting attitude again, Rourke's balance gone. Still holding the Soviet pilot, Rourke fell back. The pilot's left crashed across John Rourke's face, impacting Rourke over the cheekbone, and Rourke's head slammed against the fuselage.

Rourke's grip loosened.

The pilot tore away from him, a right and then a left, Rourke feebly blocking them.

The pilot bent over, wrenching the knife from the decking, then ramming it down and forward in a dagger thrust for John Rourke's chest.

John Rourke wheeled left, losing his balance as he kicked, his right leg sweeping against the pilot's left knee, the knife leaving the pilot's hand, stabbing into the bulkhead fabric as Rourke's left fist rose up, catching the pilot on the right side tip of the jaw, the Soviet pilot's head and neck and back arching away, spilling into the open fuselage doorway, a look of terror in the man's eyes. And then the gunship lurched once more and the body sailed outward and the fuselage door slammed and there wasn't even a scream.

John Rourke sank to his knees, the gunship's attitude to the ground changing again, the door slapping back open. The pilot was gone.

John Rourke was up, half falling forward, grasping for the pilot's seat, slumping into it.

Through the chin bubble, he could see ground, jagged and rocky. Rourke's hands clenched around the joystick. Autopilot. There was a disengage switch.

His head swam with nausea and pain.

He shook his head.

John Rourke reached up. The red switch to disengage autopilot. He flipped the toggle. It broke.

"Shit!"

The gunship was skimming low across the ground now, the starboard ski tearing through a pine tree, branches hurtled up into the main rotor overhead, shredding as they sprayed over the Plexiglas surrounding him.

The joystick still wouldn't respond.

Rourke's right fist punched upward into the autopilot control panel.

Rourke tried the joystick again.

A missile contrail crossed his nose, the gunship vibrating from the slipstream.

Another gunship, tongues of flame licking from its miniguns.

The fingers of John Rourke's left hand found the haft of the LS-X knife and he ripped it from the leather. "Damn you!"

Rourke stabbed the knife into the overhead autopilot panel, sparks of electricity arcing across the blade as his right hand reached for the joystick.

He had control.

Rourke left the knife where it was, his eyes scanning for the weapons console. "There!" A second chopper crossed his nose and mini-guns blazed toward him, a spiderwebbing gouge across the chin bubble below him, but the integrity of the Plexiglas still holding.

Missiles.

Armed.

John Rourke shifted targeting to manual from auto.

The portside package.

Rourke took the gunship down, then hauled on the joystick, the gunship rising as Rourke arced it around a full one hundred eighty degrees, one of the two gunships after him making a pass. Rourke engaged one from the portside package, then another, the contrails crisscrossing each other as they homed toward the target.

The second gunship was coming in fast and dead on.

John Rourke took his gunship into a dive as the first of the two enemy ships exploded, a fireball washing across the air above him.

Snow and ice pelted against his windshield, the windshield wipers working furiously now.

Mini-guns blazed toward him, Rourke activating a rearward-firing missile as he skimmed over the treetops.

His mouth was bleeding from the fistfight.

A missile contrail skimmed beneath him and he climbed, realized it was a mistake, started the dive as the second contrail arced over his nose.

The corners of John Rourke's mouth turned up. He was tired, hungry for real food—and frightened more than he ever had been in his life because of Natalia.

"Eat it," Rourke almost whispered.

The terrain followed, then rotated one hundred eighty

degrees and started to climb. The remaining Soviet gunship was coming for him, dead on, mini-guns firing. A missile contrail.

John Rourke's finger rested over the last of his aft-firing portside missiles.

He let the machine turn one hundred eighty degrees, tail rotor facing the enemy, and touched fire control, the gunship vibrating, Rourke starting the machine into a dive as he looked back.

A missile contrail passed over him.

A missile contrail was vectoring for the last gunship's underbelly.

The air seemed to pulse with the explosion.

# Chapter Eighteen

Akiro Kurinami's readout indicated that he would be impacting the west wall of the canyon with the tips of his main rotor blades in ten seconds, but if he slipped to starboard, he'd do the same on the opposite side. And his instincts told him he would make it.

He followed his instincts.

"Set your guidance computers to my exact coordinates. Do not deviate," he had told the men of his squadron as he had revealed his plan for the raid along the canyon route to the south of the Soviet staging area. He would soon find out if they had listened.

The readouts were set, after all, to provide a margin for error.

His hands were balled tight on the controls, his knuckles almost white.

Snow was falling heavily here, but the swirling snow helped him to read better the eddying updrafts and downdrafts of the canyon.

He judged it would be five minutes or less until they came in range of the machine gun batteries and the surface-to-air missiles which haphazardly guarded this unlikely approach to the staging area for the gunships. And until the first shots were exchanged, radio silence had to be maintained.

If his squadron had listened, they would make it through.

There was not enough maneuvering room between the

canyon walls to employ missiles safely from the weapons pods against the emplacements. It would be guns only.

He was terrain-following with the German gunship, but laterally as well as in elevation, an outcropping of rock suddenly appearing, all his senses immediately responding as he made minute course adjustments, always going forward, the estimated distance to the defensive positions guarding the canyon approach now only three minutes away.

He could not take his eyes from the canyon long enough to double-check his guns. Kurinami called to his doorgunner, but by voice only. "Corporal—be ready! As soon as firing begins, slide that door open and take whatever targets of opportunity present themselves. After we have passed by the defensive positions, reload quickly, because we will be encountering heavy resistance within minutes and be almost directly over the staging area."

"Yes, Herr Lieutenant!"

Kurinami's head ached with the strain; he was afraid even to blink.

One minute at the outside now.

He could not look back to be certain the other machines of his squadron were still with him. Radio silence could not yet be broken.

He tried to flex his fingers, but almost allowed a slip to port that would have been disastrous. He was flying for all of them if their instruments were on him as they should be.

The minute was up. At any second—

He heard the whoosh of the missile and reacted, shouting into his headset as he took what evasive action he could, "This is Retribution Leader. I am under attack from the east side of the canyon rim. Attack! Attack! Stand by!" Kurinami's starboard machine guns. He swept them over the canyon wall and over the rim, the missile exploding in mid-air perhaps fifty yards away, a muted shout from the German corporal who was his doorgunner. Kurinami started to climb, cutting over to intraship on his headset. "Corporal!"

"I am all right, Herr Lieutenant!"

And there was a sudden roar as the fuselage integrity was compromised by the open door, a rush of cold air sweeping in. Kurinami shivered.

Machine-gun fire impacted the rock wall to the west, another missile contrail. Kurinami started climbing, still not enough maneuvering room to use his own missiles. But these surface-to-air missiles weren't that terribly fast. He targeted the missile with his guns, then led it, then fired, the enemy missile exploding in mid-air dead ahead of him as he wrenched at the controls, leapfrogging over it.

He changed pitch, sweeping up out of the canyon near its west wall, an updraft catching him, almost losing it, rotating ninety degrees and crossing over the canyon, intentionally exposing himself so the others behind him could get the elevation needed to maneuver and respond.

Another missile. Kurinami began evasive action, radically altering pitch into a dive for the east-side rim, one of the machine-gun emplacements visible. Kurinami hit fire control for one of the forward-firing missiles on the portside pod, the gunship's frame vibrating with it for an instant, the contrail streaking toward the emplacement. Already, Kurinami was rising. A missile impacted the canyon wall just below him, at the very edge of the rim, great boulders and clouds of granite dust belching upward, Kurinami going for elevation.

One of his squadron was in trouble, smoke billowing from the tail rotor, control visibly going. Kurinami banked to starboard and started into a dive.

Machine-gun fire was ripping across the already partially crippled chopper's fuselage. Kurinami acquired the emplacement's coordinates and opened fire with his own guns, sweeping over the emplacement, snow and rocks plowing upward in a wake under his guns, something near the emplacement exploding, Kurinami climbing his machine to get away from it.

Another of the German gunships rose up from inside the

canyon walls and fired a missile, the missile battery that was its apparent target exploding, a huge yellow and orange fireball rising, missiles tracking erratically out of the flames.

"This is Retribution Leader. Retribution four is going down on the west rim. Number three—pick up. One and two stay on me and proceed to primary objective. Retribution Leader out."

In seconds, he expected the first of the Soviet gunships to come over the horizon line.

The snow was as heavy as it had been, his instruments showing an increase in windspeed. "Corporal?"

"Yes, Herr Lieutenant?"

"Be ready."

"Yes, Herr Lieutenant."

And Kurinami heard the action cycling on the doorgun.

# Chapter Nineteen

The rotor blades stirred lazily over them, snow swirling in little cyclonic formations around them. John Rourke's best friend stood before him. "You dropped this," Paul Rubenstein offered, smiling, handing over the lost Scoremaster. But the smile looked somehow forced. "It doesn't look any the worse for wear. Dug it out of about a foot and a half of snow." The Detonics .45, indeed, seemed almost miraculously unscathed, Rourke's eyes quickly scanning its exterior in the green light from the Soviet gunship's control panels and overheads. But when one considered the heavy snow covering the ground and its cushioning effect on a falling object, it was more understandable. And the Detonics pistols were notoriously well-made, from the best materials.

John Rourke took the gun in his fist, grateful that Paul had been able to recover it, Rourke's hands moving over it. "Thank you," and he turned toward Natalia.

She was standing up, laughing hysterically, but with a vacant look in her eyes that was maddening, her eye color perverted by the lights from the gunship.

Rourke's eyes drifted down to the .45's rear sight, his fingers moving over it, Natalia's laughter creeping through him. And he realized his hands were trembling. He told himself it was just that he was coming down off the adrenaline rush. But he knew he was lying to himself.

111

"Are you feeling better?" John Rourke asked Natalia Tiemerovna.

She laughed, the laughter unbroken, not a response but a continuation.

Rourke looked at Paul Rubenstein. "Help me with her. We'll fly across the gorge and get Otto picked up, then show me that designated rendezvous. We can plot the most likely course between where you left them and the rendezvous and backtrack until we pick them up. Tell Otto we're on the way," Rourke concluded, "and I'll get Natalia started."

The younger man nodded, pulling on his helmet to use the radio headset more conveniently, John Rourke walking slowly toward Natalia, his palms open as though approaching a threatened animal. And at once she stopped laughing, pulling her knees up close against her chest, her arms hugged around them, her face angled away from him, almost as if she somehow anticipated he would strike her. "We have to go and get Annie and Michael now. Isn't it great to see Paul? Did he tell you Michael was all right?"

But Natalia, still hugging her knees, only began laughing again . . .


John Rourke sat at the controls of the Soviet gunship, Paul Rubenstein beside him, Natalia's laughter all but subsided, a sedative from the medical kit of one of the Specials quieting her.

"What are you going to do, John?" Paul Rubenstein asked him.

Rourke clenched one of the thin, dark tobacco cigars unlit in his teeth, terrain-following with the Soviet helicopter, his left hand searching his pockets for the battered Zippo windlighter. But he remembered it was without fuel. "You don't have a match, do you?"

"You?"

"I don't like using Lifeboat Matches just to light a cigar. And these Russian choppers don't come with a cigar lighter."

"Otto?" Rubenstein began, twisting around in his seat, calling across the fuselage, "got a light for John?"

"Certainly!" In the next moment, Hammerschmidt was leaning between them, a cigarette going in his mouth as he cupped a lighter in his hands, John Rourke thrusting the end of the cigar just above the flame, drawing it upward into the tobacco.

"Thank you," Rourke murmured.

"How much longer until we intersect their line of travel, Herr Doctor?"

Rourke smiled. As often as he told Hammerschmidt to call him "John" or just "Rourke" and as often as Hammerschmidt would, the German commando captain more often reverted to formal address. "I think we'll hit it in another fifteen minutes if the winds don't pick up or the storm doesn't worsen." The windshield wipers clicked and clacked back and forth relentleslsy and snow was wedged where it had some protection against their slipstream, the wedges growing.

"If you do not need me, I shall try to sleep a bit, then."

"Go for it," Rourke nodded, exhaling a thin stream of gray smoke through each nostril.

As Hammerschmidt moved away, Rourke looked at Paul beside him. "I don't know what I'm going to do about Natalia. I know she can't go without more help than we can give her. And with everything around us falling apart, there's a limit to where I can safely take her. Mid-Wake, maybe. Or maybe New Germany. I'm going to check with Dr. Munchen as soon as we get out of here and see what he recommends. He was very impressed with Mid-Wake's medical technology and he knows what New Germany has to offer. And I trust him. You agree?"

"Yeah. What, ahh—"

Rourke smiled, but inside he felt burned out, hollow, and from the reaction evident in Paul Rubenstein's eyes, it showed. "Do I have a prognosis?"

"Yes—a prognosis—I guess."

John Rourke's eyes returned to the storm, consulted the windshield, then the terrain-following radar, then the windshield again. "Doctors don't use crystal balls, and as far as this is concerned I'm little more qualified to hazard a guess than the average layman. I've got some training in recognizing symptoms, I've got the vocabulary, I don't have the skills. And if I did, I'm too close to her. And I'm the cause of the problem—"

"That's bullshit, John—"

"No—but thanks." And Rourke exhaled smoke through his nostrils again, the smoke dissipating on the streams of air from the forward ventilation blowers. "You know exactly what I mean. More than anybody besides Natalia and me, you know."

"So—what? You saying that because you're an honorable man and you wouldn't cheat on your wife, you did something wrong? I mean—my God!"

"I'm saying that what happened wouldn't have happened if it hadn't been for me. That's what I'm saying. I broke it, and I'm going to fix it." And he intended to do that, no matter what it meant.

# Chapter Twenty

Gunships rose ahead of him, a black wall only brought into existence, Kurinami realized, to give the appearance of impenetrability. It gave that appearance indeed.

"Retribution Three—this is Retribution Leader. Status report. Over."

"This is Retribution Three, Retribution Leader. Crew of Retribution Four safely aboard. Doorgunner sustained minor injuries. We are coming up behind you. Over."

"Prepare to execute Attack Plan Three—I repeat, Attack Plan Three. Do all other elements copy? Over."

"This is Retribution One, Retribution Leader. I copy. Over."

"This is Retribution Two, Retribution Leader. Copy that. Over."

"This is Retribution Three, Retribution Leader. Affirmative. Attack Plan Three. Over."

"This is Retribution Leader," Kurinami whispered into the teardrop-shaped microphone just before his lips. "Execute—I say again, execute. Retribution Leader out!" Kurinami changed main rotor pitch and banked the machine sharply to starboard, coming about ninety degrees and climbing, the phalanx of Soviet gunships breaking up into a less than imaginative-looking evasive plan if he read their maneuver correctly. "Retribution Two—on your tail. Do you copy?"

"I copy, Retribution Leader. Over." Retribution Two

rotated a full one hundred eighty degrees and fired missiles from port and starboard forward-facing weapons pods, the Soviet gunship that had come up under it vaporizing in the instant the missile contrail crossed.

Strafing fire crossed the nose of Kurinami's machine at the level of the chin bubble, Kurinami banking to starboard and climbing again, coming about one hundred eighty degrees and firing his starboard mini-guns, the enemy gunship's tail rotor spinning away from its mounting, the Soviet machine rotating uncontrollably on its axis, climbing and diving. If the Soviet were a good pilot, he might be able to land it, but the machine was out of action.

Kurinami ignored the gunship. Killing was for assassins.

He banked his machine to port and dove, Retribution Three coming down into a hover at the center of the enemy gunship pack, rotating on the axis of its main rotor and firing fore and aft missiles, then changing pitch and diving to port, Soviet mini-guns firing into their own machines, others of the Soviet machines exploding.

Kurinami redlined his craft, banking to port, firing forward missiles from both pods. Another two of the enemy gunships were gone.

At the edges of his peripheral vision, he saw them coming, aerial mines hurtling downward on small parachutes from a Soviet craft above him. If one should contact even the tip of a rotor blade— Kurinami dove, changing pitch, banking to starboard, under two of the Soviet gunships, machine-gun fire etching across the bubble, disabling one of the wiper blades.

The corporal who was his drafted doorgunner was firing, stitching machine-gun fire into a Soviet gunship coming off the west rim of the canyon. A hit into the fuel system, the gunship exploding, consumed now in a black and orange fireball, the fireball rising in the canyon updraft.

Kurinami's German gunship rocked as one of the mines contacted one of the Soviet machines.

Kurinami's vision through the bubble obscured now, snow

116

icing over it, he started to climb, another of the Soviet gunships taking a hit from one of the aerial mines, its tail section blowing in two, the machine plummeting downward leaving a tail of fire.

Retribution One was coming down out of the low-hanging snowclouds, firing aft-facing missiles, two Soviet gunships in close pursuit. Kurinami banked to starboard and dove on them, saying into his radio, "Retribution One—Gunther! They are on you!"

One of the Soviet gunships exploded, a direct hit to the underside of the fuselage, the other aft-firing missile from Retribution One sputtering away, lost in the cloudbank. But Retribution One was on fire. The second Soviet gunship was closing.

Kurinami checked his weapons status. Most of his remaining missiles were aft-firing. "Damnit!" Kurinami banked to port and interposed his own machine between Retribution One and the Soviet gunship. As Kurinami fired, the Soviet gunship fired as well.

"Gunther—get down and away from your machine!"

Kurinami felt the vibration rattling through him, heard the rattle of his corporal's doorgun, saw the fireball behind him as the Soviet aircraft took the missile hit and exploded, felt his ears ringing as there was a scream, then the scream was cut off in the loudest sound he had ever heard.

Kurinami looked back.

The doorgunner—"My God!"—was impaled, a shrapnel fragment through his chest and throat, eyes wide open beneath his goggles, fire starting in the tail section, spreading forward as the open fuselage door fanned it.

Kurinami started down, already losing some control from his tail rotor.

Retribution Three flew past. Kurinami's radio came alive. "This is Retribution Three, Retribution Leader. I will follow you down."

"Negative! Negative! Follow Retribution One down. We

have them on the run. But there is no time for both of us. I know this countryside. I will be all right. I have the portable radio and survival kit and I am armed. You have your orders."

There would be barely time to get Gunther and his doorgunner from Retribution One, barely time before the Soviet gunships reassembled, then counterattacked.

The ground was coming up fast.

Kurinami felt for the Beretta in the holster at his side, his bag with the heavy coat strapped to it. His eyes flickered up— the fire extinguisher, his only way out. The fuselage wall-mounted survival kit. He knew its contents. German survival knife, emergency food, first aid kit, fire starting and signaling devices. A solar battery radio.

Kurinami had lost ninety percent of tail rotor control, and the fuel line off the main tank was spraying now, the part of the bubble he could see through because the wiper blade still worked slicking over.

The fire—he could smell it—advancing. But there was no time to look around.

The ground.

Kurinami banked, the machine responding slowly. He was crashing toward the canyon wall. He cut tail rotor power and immediately the craft began to spin.

He changed pitch radically, the gunship slipping away from the canyon wall at a sickening angle.

He braced himself.

Impact.

Akiro Kurinami shook his head, hit the quick release on his seat restraint, reached for the extinguisher.

Flames gushed toward him as he fell against the control panels, aiming the extinguisher at their base, spraying. The fire retreated a foot or so.

He reached for his bag, had it. The survival kit. Had it.

Kurinami sprayed the base of the flames again, running, hurtling over what he realized was his doorgunner's burning body, his right shoulder impacting the door flange, his left

118

jumpsuit leg aflame.

He shot out the last of the extinguisher's contents against his leg as he half fell, half jumped from the machine. He rolled across the snow, heaping whole handfuls of it over his left trouser leg.

He was up, slipped, grabbed the bag and the survival kit and ran, feeling the heat rush and the slap of air pressure against him, his footing going. The explosion roared through his head as he fell.

# Chapter Twenty-One

Sarah Rourke somehow felt better about herself. It was always better to be useful. And, with the borrowed German Battle Dress Utilities (the coat open) she barely looked pregnant. As much as her daughter, Annie, favored skirts and dresses, she herself had always taken every chance she could to get into a comfortable pair of Levi's or something similar.

She remembered her high school days. Like all the other girls she went to school with, she had longed to be able to wear pants in the winter and shorts when the weather was warm, but the dress code—no pants, no shorts, skirts or dresses so much below the knee.

There had never been a dress code for Annie, and maybe that was why. And for Annie, for all she had known then the only female actually living on the surface of the earth (she, Sarah, and Natalia were in the Sleep), attire had become a means of identity.

Sarah Rourke picked up her German gunbelt. The holster was a big fit for her Trapper Scorpion .45, but a safe carry. She buckled the belt on, and even with the bulge the baby made, the belt was a comfortable fit.

She walked to the entry flap of the tent, opened it and passed through the airlock.

Colonel Wolfgang Mann and a dozen German commandoes, men like Otto Hammerschmidt who she wished was going to be with them, waited for her.

"Frau Rourke. If I may say so," Colonel Mann began, bowing slightly as he smiled, "our field uniform looks most appealing on you."

"Thank you. I'm ready now."

"Very well, Frau Rourke." And Mann turned to address his men, doing so in English out of respect for her, she realized; but since all of the men seemed to be either officers or senior noncoms, it was wholly likely their knowledge of English wasn't being strained. "Frau Rourke will guide us after we penetrate the section of the First Chinese City which is now controlled by the Soviets. It is reasonable to assume that some chance exists that the chairman of the Chinese Republic was taken there after his capture. Other friendly force personnel may be held prisoner there as well." He removed a cigarette case from beneath his uniform blouse.

"We must assume," Mann went on, lighting a cigarette after offering one to her that she declined, "that our adversaries will not hesitate to execute hostages, most particularly the chairman himself. Since the Herr Chairman was under German protection at the time of his capture, his capture is indeed a German responsibility. This condition must be rectified. Once inside the facility, Frau Rourke will conduct our tour, as it were, until we confirm the location of what hostages may be present and have correlated the needed details to effect their rescue and to retake the facility. There are questions?"

There were no questions.

He turned to her. "Frau Rourke—if you would be so good as to accompany me then. I believe our aircraft and a small force of Chinese soldiers await."

She took his offered arm, feeling ludicrous doing it dressed as she was.

But she also felt excited.

# Chapter Twenty-Two

Annie Rubenstein stopped the Special and gazed skyward toward the sound she had thought she'd heard. She pulled her helmet off, her hair cascading to her shoulders, wisps of her hair blowing across her face in the stiff, icy cold wind. She shook her hair and the wind caught it, taking it away from her face.

Through the swirling snow, she saw the black shape.

A Soviet gunship.

"Shit!"

Catching up her hair and packing it into the helmet as she pulled it on, she glanced back once again.

From the rifle boot on the Special, she pulled her M-16, worked the charging handle, set the selector to safe, then rammed it back into the boot, securing the cover only so she wouldn't lose it.

Her hands gripped the handlebars and she gunned the Special, starting off across the windswept side of the defile, the snow vastly less deep here and more navigable.

The helicopter was fully audible now.

With an earsplitting crack, it raced over her, momentarily darkening the pre-dawn gray to black.

The helicopter turned a full one hundred eighty degrees, hovering over the trail. Annie accelerated, nearly fifty miles per hour now, the gunship following over her.

A voice came over the helicopter.

Annie looked up.

"Stop your vehicle!" The words were in Russian and she'd learned a little of that from Natalia, studied it more in Lydveldid Island.

She gunned the Special ahead, over sixty now, the bike handling well but not made for speeds like this on terrain like this.

"Stop or be fired upon!"

She kept going.

The helicopter passed her, hovering so low over the ground she couldn't pass under it, snow swirling around it in great clouds, cyclonically. She veered the Special right, toward the higher ground, less snow there still. But the side of the defile was shaley, the Special slipping laterally, her feet out, bracing the machine. She kept going.

"You will stop your machine or be shot!"

She reached to the rifle boot, almost losing the machine, but kept it going.

The Soviet gunship skipped over her, so close the slipstream around it nearly ripped her from the saddle.

A roar like that of some sort of wounded beast back in the days when there were beasts besides those which masqueraded as men. She kept going, the roar louder, mini-guns gouging across the path over which she took the Special. She had to veer from the path, twisting the fork hard left, almost losing control. But as she gained full control, her right arm passed through the sling of the M-16, her right fist closed over the pistol grip of the five-centuries-old Colt assault rifle, her thumb working the selector to full auto, her right arm thrusting upward. She fired into the underside of the Soviet gunship's fuselage. It was armored, she knew. But she wasn't about to die without firing a shot.

The gunship banked sharply and disappeared over the ridgeline.

Annie knew she'd bought time.

She safed the M-16, letting it fall to her side on its sling as she had seen her father do so many times. She wanted to shout for him or for Paul—she thought of her father, of Natalia.

She increased her speed, seventy-five now, the machine bumping and twisting over the rough terrain.

The gunship. "Damn you!" She raised the M-16, almost losing control, stabbed it toward the Soviet gunship's chin bubble, fired out half the magazine. Still the gunship came, coming right at her.

The mini-guns plowed furrows on both sides of her. She let go of the M-16, the rifle slapping against her right thigh.

The helicopter's downdraft of swirling snow would have blinded her except for the face shield built into the helmet. It passed lower over her this time and she almost lost her nerve, almost lost the bike. She didn't.

Her fist gripped the M-16 again and she rammed it toward the gunship, firing in a ragged, upthrusting line, toward the main rotor, but the odds of hitting anything were more than remote, ludicrous.

Ahead of her, the ground broke. Annie Rourke Rubenstein twisted the fork right and made for it, not knowing what lay beyond, but hoping for cover. The M-16 swung empty and temporarily useless at her side.

The ground did more than break—there was a drop. She didn't know how far. Annie threw all her body weight into the fork, feet going to the ground, soles dragging over the shale, bulldogging her machine to the ground, dragging it back as it started over the lip of a precipice. She fell, the M-16's sling slipping from her shoulder.

She shook her head, the helmet falling from her head as she forced herself to her knees.

Her right hand grabbed for the butt of the Detonics Scoremaster.

To her feet. She stumbled, staggered, shook her head to clear it. Her left hand closed on the butt of the military Beretta.

The gunship was bearing down on her, mini-guns blazing, the ground ahead of her ripping up in waves. She thrust both pistols toward the gunship, hissing, "Eat lead, you Commie—"

And there was a sound so loud that her ears rang with it and the ground seemed to shake, the Soviet gunship veering north, climbing, the sky darkening. Her body shook as she looked up. Directly above her, not more than fifty feet, hovered a second Soviet gunship.

She raised both pistols to fire at it.

A voice came over the speaker. "Annie—it's me, and your father!"

It was her husband's voice. "Paul!"

The gunship shot forward and touched ground, Paul darting from the opening gunner's door, ducking his head as the gunship slipped left across the ground and rose almost straight upward.

Paul ran toward her. She ran toward him and he took her into his arms. "Thank God you're alive," she shouted.

"Get to cover!" And he was dragging her now, the guns still in her hands, her eyes not watching as she ran, but looking back toward the gunship. It had to be her father or Natalia at the controls. She had memorized the black shape's registry numbers, would know it when the other gunship— It was back.

They hovered, hundreds of feet above the ground, like two bulls pawing at the ground preparing to charge each other in some fight to the death. She had seen a bullfight once in a movie her father stored on videotape.

Paul was still dragging her and he dragged her down, holding her tight against him, both her hands still holding her pistols, her eyes riveted to the sky.

The Soviet gunship that had harassed her, meant to kill her, moved first, a missile launched, the contrail moving straight as an arrow or a beam of light, moving straight for the gunship piloted by— "Is Daddy at the controls?"

"Yes. Cover your ears."

She obeyed, but she watched, the second gunship, the one her father flew, already out of sight, the missile impacting the side of the defile, a shower of rock spraying upward, raining downward.

Her father's gunship was suddenly back, rising from behind the wall of the defile, firing one missile, rotating one hundred eighty degrees, launching an aft-firing missile, the enemy gunship taking evasive action, slipping left and going for elevation, the first missile missing it cleanly, the second missile—

For an instant, the enemy gunship just seemed to stop, and then there was no gunship anymore, only a fireball, and the ground trembled and flaming debris fell and Paul drew her closer to him, his hands and arms protecting her head and upper body, her face against his chest.

# Chapter Twenty-Three

Sarah Rourke's hands trembled, the weight of the weapon she carried all that kept them from shaking violently. It was not fear; she knew that feeling; it was anticipation of action, a building adrenaline rush. She moved through the darkness behind Wolfgang Mann, the entry tunnel into the most recently exposed of the First City's "petals" without electrification and the enemy too close to risk a hand-held flashlight or other form of illumination. All of the men, Colonel Mann included, wore a type of vision-intensification goggles. She had almost chosen not to, anticipating they would be heavy and awkward, but they proved to be just the opposite, the "guts" of the system attached to the front of the uniform blouse by means of a clip and feeding up to the goggles with a thin spiraling wire much like a miniature version of a twentieth-century telephone cord. She could see clearly, and as she walked behind Wolfgang Mann, she was glad she had decided for the goggles, for their very existence made illumination unnecessary. A struck match would have appeared as bright as a beacon here. Everywhere about the tunnel debris was scattered, the dust of centuries of disuse dating from the time the First Chinese City was built as a shelter against World War Three.

The weapon she carried was one of the newest German assault rifles, these, as Mann had told her, not yet general issue. It fired the new 7.5mm caseless round from forty-round disposable magazines, the cartridges either bulleted as a conventional hardball military round—she had picked up a great deal of her husband's and son's weaponry argot since the Awakening—or the same round bulleted with impact-detonated high explosives. Beneath the primary barrel was a secondary barrel, this vented for diffusion of gas, the barrel itself fed with lock-in disposable plastic magazines utilizing self-contained, single-shot, manually operated bolt actions, the magazine carrying ten rounds of 40mm grenade-like projectiles, available projectiles at this early phase of the weapon's introduction into service only high-explosive and tear gas.

From her limited theoretical understanding of firearms—hers was only a practical understanding begat by necessity since the Night of the War—the new German weapon, labeled the STG-101, was "hot stuff." Somehow she knew her husband, despite his traditionalism, would appreciate it.

Sarah Rourke moved ahead, the STG-101's heavily checkered pistol grip tight in her right fist, the checkering so deep (yet non-abrasive) that she could feel it subtly through the black leather gloves she had been given to wear.

The STG-101's carrying handle was fitted with fully adjustable military-style sights, of the type she was used to with the centuries-old M-16s, but within the handle itself was a scope, three-power she had been told, and by utilizing a hollow cavity within the synthetic straight-line buttstock, the STG-101's scope could be battery powered, as was hers, for use as a vision-intensification scope.

But she hoped the new guns would not have to be used here, because even with the flash-suppressor, which Mann had told her was very effective, discharging of a single round would betray the firer's position.

Her radio headset was newest German field issue as well, powered by galvanic skin response, sound traveling from the set along the bones to her inner ear, voice transmitted by bone as well to the set which then transmitted to the receiving set.

Her eyes shifted from Colonel Mann's broad-set shoulders to

the robot-operated viewers ahead, fitted with miniaturized video transmitters, one of the commandoes on a steady mount suspended from his chest and shoulders monitoring the video output, like a director in a television studio punching up different shots, in complete control of the robot-operated cameras. There were two of them, neck-like appendages on the robots extending several feet upward or outward, ungainly looking, like huge sheet cakes, no more than a foot high at the base, but three feet square and mounted on miniaturized tank treads.

One of the robots was behaving oddly, if behavior were indeed the way to describe the actions of a machine. It was cutting a zig-zag pattern well ahead of the second machine, its camera tentacles—the lenses incorporated in the tentacles—extending at bizarre angles.

On the comm line she heard the video operator's voice. "Herr Colonel. Unit Two has something."

Sarah Rourke stopped, joining the cluster of men around the video operator, looking over his left forearm toward the screen on his left front. Colonel Mann was speaking, and it was an odd effect, hearing his real voice and his voice transmitted as well. "There—in the shadowy area to the right of the screen. I saw it again."

"A man?" She spoke without thinking, and all the others turned toward her.

"Yes, Frau Rourke," Colonel Mann agreed. "But who? You will stay here—"

"No," she said, "I can carry my weight." And she thought of her swelling abdomen. Her weight was getting more considerable all the time.

"Very well. You two will come with us. You will keep the video monitors trained on us at all times. Shall we?" And Colonel Mann turned toward her and then nodded his head forward along the tunnel.

She fell in step beside him, the STG-101 tight in her hands, one of the grenade magazines in place, one of the standard

7.5mm-ball rounds chambered. With the availability of the grenades, she had explosives if need be.

She heard Mann's voice whispering through the bones in her ear. "We must be as silent as possible, Frau Rourke."

"Call me by my first name, please. You're making me feel like I'm a thousand years old instead of just five hundred." Why was she trying to make a joke, she asked herself? A little fear, yes.

"Sarah. Follow my lead. Schmidt, Mueller, take the opposite side of the tunnel. Knives if possible." And as he spoke she looked at him, Mann drawing a knife of comparatively modest size from a sheath at his right hip; by comparison to the Jack Crain knife her husband had begun carrying, had had made for him five centuries ago, any knife was modest in size.

She remembered the fight that had caused, oddly now. And yet he had saved his own life with it, Natalia had killed Karamatsov with it. "What do you need a knife that size for, John? It's the size of a sword, for God's sake."

"There are two schools of thought with knives, basically," he had begun and she had known it was going to be one of his weapons lectures and she hated them because she didn't understand them and, in those days, had thought that mere possession of weapons was tantamount to insanity. Sure, a shotgun in the house because they lived far from town, but what else did anyone need? And John had to carry a gun because of what he did for a living. But did he need all of those guns? "Some people," he'd gone on, "believe that a long-bladed knife is for showboating. You can accomplish almost any task with a knife with a blade six inches or less, seven at the outside. But a larger knife can accomplish those same tasks, usually with greater efficiency. And its formidable appearance aids in its use as a weapon if need be, not to mention the possibility of being stranded in the field with a firearm that is for some reason or another non-functional. There's the question of dangerous predators to consider, etc. But it really boils down to versatility. A large knife is more versatile than a small knife. This will be good for Michael someday."

"Why would Michael need it? Answer me that. Why would Michael need half the things you've put away for him?"

"Someday," he continued, patiently, "the mere possession of a weapon of any sort or anything that can be construed as a weapon may be so filled with legal pitfalls and restrictions that the wealth of fine firearms and edged weapons available today may be a thing of the past. If a situation arises for which a high-quality firearm or knife is the only remedy, then what? It pays to plan ahead."

He always said that. Always had.

And sometimes, when she was alone, she would think of her naiveté, realize that if he had not planned ahead, they would all be dead now, dead like the millions of others who had died as a result of the insanity they so blandly called "the Night of the War."

Wolfgang Mann's hand touched her forearm and invaded her thoughts and suddenly she realized they were even with the video-probe robots, equidistant between them.

She normally would have carried one of the Gerber MK II knives that were all but standard equipment for the Rourke family, but she had only brought her pistol in a purse, going out to meet Colonel Mann as part of a diplomatic party, not gearing up for war.

She had never been a knife-fighter anyway. She whispered as softly as she could and yet be heard, "I'll back you up."

"Yes." And he edged forward, his body in a crouch, the knife in what she knew was called a rapier hold.

She tagged after him, her thumb beside the rifle's selector, ready to move it into the burstfire mode.

Wolfgang Mann stopped.

Sarah Rourke stopped.

Movement. The voice of the video operator in the bones of her ear. "I have that figure again, Herr Colonel. It is withdrawing, but slowly. I do not think the figure has vision-intensification capabilities."

There was no response.

The voice again. "I see what appears to be a weapon, Herr Colonel. But, Herr Colonel, I am not sure."

They kept moving, Sarah dogging Wolfgang Mann's heels.

She saw it now, too, someone moving perhaps twenty-five yards ahead of them. A Russian? Or was it one of the Chinese sent to meet them and he'd only gotten his signals crossed? She guessed the same thoughts filled Wolfgang Mann's mind as well.

Maybe it was being pregnant, but sometimes the most ridiculous thoughts came to her mind—if Colonel Mann were going to begin calling her by her given name, then what should she call him? Wolfey? She almost giggled just at the thought of calling him that and she had never been a giggler; but pregnancy did weird things with hormones.

Mann moved ahead quickly now and Sarah picked her way after him.

He broke into a noiseless run. She ran, too, the new German assault rifle suddenly heavy in her hands, her palms sweating inside the gloves through which she held it.

Mann dodged right, into the center of the tunnel, and the mysterious figure started to run. The voice of the remote video operator came again. "That is a weapon. The profile looks Russian. Be careful, Herr Colonel!"

There was a blinding flash but only for an instant, the vision-intensification goggles self-compensating, she had been told. She had already squinted her eyes shut against the flash as she heard the concussion of the shot, ringing in the confined area of the tunnel, reverberating off the tunnel walls and floor and ceiling.

As she opened her eyes, Colonel Mann was tackling the figure with the gun, the gun discharging again, but in a different direction, the flash less blindingly bright, Sarah throwing the STG-101 to her shoulder, shouting now, "Colonel—Wolfgang!"

But there was no clear shot as Mann bulldogged the figure to the tunnel floor, more shots discharging into the ceiling, the whining of the ricochets maddeningly loud.

Sarah ran, stumbled, almost fell, caught herself.

Mann was on his knees, and she realized both Mann and the figure who had fired were wrestling over Mann's knife.

The two commandoes, Schmidt and Mueller, were running up to aid their commanding officer, but she was closest.

The figure with whom Colonel Mann struggled was too big to be Chinese, she told herself—had to be Russian.

She summoned up images of every John Wayne movie she'd ever seen as she inverted the still-safed battle rifle in her hands, grasping it where the front stock ended. She swung, the rifle seeming to hesitate in mid-swing for an instant, a loud cracking sound then and the Russian or whoever it was fell back, groaning in pain, rolling about on the tunnel floor, hands clasped over his face.

Colonel Mann was on him, fists hammering across the lower jaw. And then Colonel Mann sagged back on his haunches, brushing dust from his uniform.

He looked up at her, smiling like some sort of little boy fresh from a schoolyard scuffle. "You saved my life—Sarah. He was stronger than I, this fellow. Let us see who he is, shall we?"

She was still holding onto the rifle as if it were a broom.

How far she'd come from when she wouldn't have known the way to hold a rifle at all, Sarah Rourke thought . . .


When Akiro Kurinami finally shrugged into the coat, he was freezing from drying sweat. But it was the first moment he had been able to stop, on a headlong lunge along the canyon wall, even hiding impossible, just running since his aircraft had been shot down and his doorgunner killed. A brave young man. And if he made it out alive, Kurinami promised himself, he would let the young man's family know just how brave. But even now, despite the coat and the time since he had donned it, Akiro Kurinami was still chilled to the marrow.

133

The air over the battle scene had been thick with Soviet gunships one instant, then nothing the next as they had pursued the remaining gunships of his force. But such a serious blow had been struck the Soviet armada, he doubted seriously that another attack against Eden Base and the German base near it could be launched without heavy reinforcement.

The Soviet gunships were gone, but the canyon walls surrounding and the ground above which the gunship battle had taken place were all but crawling with Soviet personnel, many of them commandoes of the Elite Corps.

Midway along the canyon floor, exhaustion had finally taken over, Kurinami's lungs burning with it, and he had searched the canyon's sides for some place that would afford a modicum of concealment from aerial or ground observation.

It was a wide cleft in tall rocks on which he finally settled, one of the rocks, perhaps centuries ago, pushed over by some enormous force, and now reclining against the other, forming a natural roof over him.

A quick assessment of the items rescued from the about-to-explode aircraft included one Beretta 92F military pistol (U.S. M-9), two spare fifteen-round magazines, one German survival knife with about an eight-inch blade shaped more like a machete than a knife blade, one first aid kit, complete, one tube shelter with pressure-activated warming bands running through it in circular bands which would activate as soon as the shelter was opened, one liquid-filled compass, two chemical lightsticks, three packets of rations, enough to keep a man going on a light diet for three days if he did not mind what food looked like; Kurinami had seen the contents of these food packets only once and that had been enough.

There were various little gimmick items but, other than these, the only other truly useful items were a plastic cannister of survival matches, a magnesium stick to be used for shavings when fire-making materials might be damp and a plastic signal mirror.

He secured the survival kit in with his own gear, his maps, his manuals. He was tempted to burn the pilot's manuals rather than let them fall into Soviet hands, but a fire, aside from alerting the Russians to his presence, would have consumed precious matches, and to dig a hole in the rocky ground deep enough in which to bury the manuals would have been impossible.

It was time to move, to try to make it back toward friendly lines.

"Try" was the operative word.

# Chapter Twenty-Four

Michael Rourke, Maria Leuden, Han Lu Chen and the Soviet officer who was the new operations head of the KGB Elite Corps, Vassily Prokopiev, approached the natural rock chimney, the wind howling almost more loudly up from the chimney than around it, despite the hour the sky dark with the heavy, snowladen gray clouds.

"This was discovered years ago when one of our agents was captured and used it to escape the Second City and its demons," Han Lu Chen shouted over the wind. "But he was seized with madness afterward, perhaps from the howling of the winds through the chimney. But who can say? He spoke of this place, spoke of climbing for what seemed forever, and then seeing the stars."

"'Seized with madness'?" Michael queried.

"Drugs administered to him, threats of torture and the torture itself. He died shortly after achieving his freedom. What lies below the chimney is uncertain except that in some way it is connected to the interior of the Second City."

Michael Rourke studied Han's dark eyes for a moment longer, then reached up to his head, pulled back his parka and tore away the dressing, leaving only the adhesive-taped bandage over his headwound now. Maria's face seemed to show her visibly wincing. "We don't have much time. We don't know how much time, really, at all." And he addressed himself to Prokopiev. "In your condition—"

"I can climb well enough to descend."

"What about getting out, then?"

"We will never get out. You know that and so do I. So do all of us. The question raises an academic concern."

Maria Leuden's eyes were watering. Michael told himself it was the wind, only the wind causing the condition.

And then he picked up the first of the ropes.

# Chapter Twenty-Five

John Rourke stroked the blade of the Life Support System X over the sharpening stone while his daughter spoke, Natalia comfortably sedate, asleep, Otto Hammerschmidt smoking a cigarette, Paul Rubenstein staring into what passed for a fire, the Soviet equivalent of the German heater/cooker units. The unit, glowing yellow-orange, was at the center of their group, about a hundred yards from the cammie-netted helicopter gunship, beneath a natural rock outcropping, what little daylight there was barely noticeable under the bleakness of the heavy gray clouds that seemed to produce a never-ending supply of heavy, wet snow.

"So Maria made an educated guess. That if the people of the Second City worship a missile as a symbol of their god, they'd in effect call on their god to save them or avenge them, then launch the missile," Annie concluded.

"After all these centuries, it would be a long countdown. The missile would have to be fueled and the original fuel might very likely have chemically decomposed if it weren't stored in just the right manner. There could be all sorts of problems that a computer program—which has to be the only feasible means of achieving a launch under the circumstances—would have to deal with. And all that presupposes the missile's fuel lines and everything else about it are still functional. But with the proper program and the proper 'religious attendants' to service the needs of the program, I suppose it could be done."

"We didn't kill enough people the first time?" Paul Rubenstein murmured rhetorically.

"I gather not," Rourke answered anyway. "But no one there is like us. No one really remembers."

"Like you," Otto Hammerschmidt said suddenly. "Like all of you, you mean. Not even the Eden Project survivors remember. All they remember is going to sleep just as it was about to begin, then awakening when it was all over. All of you are the only ones."

"Some few of the Russians," Annie volunteered, "who took the Sleep with Karamatsov. They remember the Night of the War and everything afterward. I think Antonovitch is one of them and he's their new commander."

"The new Imperious Leader?" Paul interjected, a note of sarcasm in his voice.

"Indeed." John Rourke nodded, feeling a smile cross his lips. When was the last time he had smiled?

"But Michael and I were still children," Annie went on. "We saw things as children see them. Maybe we were luckier, luckier than the adults who saw their whole world end."

"I read of it from both sides," Otto Hammerschmidt began, as if talking to himself, his eyes seeming to follow the rising of the gray smoke from his cigarette. "The official accounts, and then the things we weren't supposed to read. About the world before. It was madness that made it happen."

"Madness begets madness," Rourke observed. "Everyone wanted everything, and they wanted it for absolutely nothing. And no one wanted the responsibility for keeping things working, for guarding the basic things about humanity that were worth saving. It had to be someone else's job, someone who was stupid enough to take the risks. Terrorism went largely unchecked. The nuclear arsenals had been stepped down. But no one addressed the problems which had caused the buildup in nuclear weapons to begin with. And no one searched for the common thread underlying the multiplicity of terrorist causes. The savagery that had existed ever since man became man was still there, only expressed in different ways. BDUs replaced animal skins, assault rifles replaced battle axes. Nuclear arsenals replaced barbarian hordes. The savagery existed. It was ignored while everyone went on with their lives just as if it weren't there at all. And while the major powers realized there was the potential for global destruction, the minor powers realized it too and that they could use this potential to their own advantage. Yeah, it was madness. Another name for it was 'humanity.'"

Rourke saw Annie looking at him oddly.

He knew the reason for the look.

His knife stoned, Rourke wiped lubricant over it lightly. "We have to solve two problems immediately. The helicopter has to get out of here with Natalia and get her to some at least reasonably safe location where she can begin to receive treatment. Michael and his party will need support if they're going up against the Second City in an attempt to prevent them launching or just detonating a nuclear warhead. The solutions available to these problems are limited. Aside from Natalia, Otto and myself are the only two people among us who can pilot a helicopter. Which means that Otto is the logical person to fly Natalia out. Logic also dictates that he's best off not undertaking such a task alone. Annie. Paul— you both should—"

"No," Paul Rubenstein said very flatly. "You're looking at this as a potential no-win situation, so you're intentionally excluding me—"

"And me," Annie chimed in.

"You are excluded," Paul said commandingly as he looked at her. Annie's eyes hardened for an instant, but then softened, her glance the embodiment of the term "mixed emotions," Rourke thought. "But I'm not. Granted, Otto will need help; a woman is tailor-made to the situation. But you'll need help, too, John."

John Rourke looked at Paul Rubenstein. He remembered when all the others had betrayed the trust of the passengers

140

after the air crash in New Mexico and the desperate trek across the desert to seek help, only Paul Rubenstein had risen to the occasion. And ever afterward they had been friends, comrades in the true sense of the word, not its Communist perversion. "I'm very proud that you're my friend," Rourke said simply, then got to his feet. "Let's get going then, since it's settled." And John Rourke caught up his things and started for the helicopter.

# Chapter Twenty-Six

The man she had beaten half-senseless with the butt of the STG-101 assault rifle was Russian, separated from his unit, his uniform torn, a grazing wound on his left thigh, disoriented and very talkative when he was promised repatriation and given medical care. And he looked at her, while she listened to him speaking Russian (of which she could barely understand a word) and listened to one of the commandoes translating. In his eyes, when they met hers, was fear. It seemed ludicrous to suppose, but perhaps he had decided to talk because he'd been afraid they would turn him over to the crazy woman who beat people with rifles rather than shot them.

The voice of the translator—she wondered how good he was—droned on, the phrases coming in jerky bits and hard-to-relate pieces. "That he was—he was part of a machine-gun crew. Yes. They set up a defensive perimeter after taking one of the—I don't know the word. The train that runs on one rail. But one of these stations and they were attacked from two sides and he and his friend were suddenly alone. They took to one of the train cars and got so far as the next station before the power went out, and then tried to escape, but were driven deeper into the city. His friend was killed by some person with a knife. He was already shot and he found this tunnel, then hid here. He didn't know that it was a tunnel leading out, rather thought it was part of some new construction. He didn't understand that the city was built, buried, then later gradually dug out, as he realizes now from having been forced into the tunnel deeper than he had planned, in order to evade capture. There are Chinese outside—inside—the tunnel and there are small Russian teams on search and destroy missions moving everywhere in the city. It is a slaughterhouse in there."

Sarah Rourke turned away from the translator (really more a paraphraser) and the Russian captive he spoke for and looked into the gray blackness ahead. Chinese soldiers, friendly forces, did indeed await. But so did Russian terror teams.

She knew this tactic. Small units, ready for suicide if need be, killing everyone they could find. It was just such a team that had invaded the cone of Hekla in Lydveldid Island and caused the death of her daughter-in-law, Madison, and Madison's and Michael's unborn baby.

"We should get going. Hear the rest of what he has to say later. We can't wait any longer."

Sarah Rourke looked at Wolfgang Mann. "I agree—Sarah. Yes." It was in the set of his face, visible despite the vision-intensification goggles he wore, visible despite the fact that the goggles themselves obscured his eyes from view. He knew what she was thinking.

"Schmidt. Mueller. Stay fifty yards behind the video probes. Be alert!" And he turned to the remote probe operator, his video panels switching on. "I want those things moving quickly. We have no more time to lose. Get them going quickly. The rest of you, standard formation. Take him along. If he cannot walk, make a chair and carry him. He is not to be turned over to the Chinese, as has been promised."

There was a look of panic in the Russian boy's face. And added to his natural fear, the fact that he could see virtually nothing farther away than the extent of his arm because he had no night-vision equipment. For a moment, she felt sympathy for him. And she felt guilt because her heart should be hardened to him.

143

She turned away and chose not to look at him again. She blamed her feelings on her pregnancy. "Stupid."

"Frau Rourke?"

"Sarah."

"Sarah. What is stupid?"

"I am; we are; they are. Stupid," she told Wolfgang Mann.

# Chapter Twenty-Seven

Otto Hammerschmidt was not the smoothest flier in the world, Paul Rubenstein decided, but seemed more than adequate to the task at hand. And the moaning emanating from Natalia was like the sounds of a restless sleeper, not displeasure with the ride. Her head lay across Annie's lap, over a blanket. Periodically, spittle dribbled from Natalia's partially open mouth and Paul Rubenstein looked away as Annie, his wife, cleaned it away. That Natalia had come to this. He shivered. Was this, perhaps, in store for them all, the pressure causing them to snap, break?

The strain of it was evident in John Rourke's ordinarily calm face, the corners of John's mouth drawn down low, his cheeks deeply seamed, the brow beneath his high forehead drawn together and down, the eyebrows arched as he alternately looked at Natalia then looked away, a look of powerlessness in his eyes that Paul Rubenstein had never seen there before, despite what normal men would have considered insurmountable odds, impossible difficulties.

Suddenly, Paul Rubenstein was consumed with a desire that he knew was insane, to take Annie away from all of this, find somewhere on earth where there was peace and just live his life there with her, raise children— He closed his eyes for an instant and when he opened them, Annie was looking at him, love in her eyes for him.

Had she read his thoughts?

Perhaps she had. He smiled at her.

Otto Hammerschmidt's voice broke the moment. "We are nearing the landing zone." Implicit in his words, though unstated, was the admonition to be ready for a quick jump-off so Hammerschmidt could get airborne again and take the liberated Soviet gunship out without being seen by either of the combatant forces.

Paul had turned his eyes forward when Hammerschmidt called to them, and now he looked back toward where Annie still cradled Natalia in her lap. John bent over Annie, kissed his daughter's forehead, then knelt beside the two women, John's right hand gently, tentatively touching Natalia's cheek. And then John bent over her troubled face, touched his lips to her cheek, then stood, walking to the fuselage door, bracing himself there, ready. For what, Paul Rubenstein wondered?

He dismissed the thoughts of what lay ahead of them, stood, making a last check of his gear; then, holding to the rope guides stretching back along the length of the fuselage, he went to Annie, knelt beside her, took her face in his hands, kissed her once, hard, on the mouth. She whispered to him, "Come back to me."

"I will," he told her, hoping he wasn't lying.

Hammerschmidt's voice called back again, that they were touching down in sixty seconds.

Paul Rubenstein looked at his wife, then at Natalia, then once again at Annie. "I will," he told her, then stood, moving more abruptly than time constraints required, joining John beside the door.

The helicopter started to settle, lurching slightly in the crosswinds of the heightening snowstorm, John wrenching the door back. The wind of their slipstream and the storm itself seemed to be sucked into the gunship as though filling a vacuum, and Paul Rubenstein fell back against it slightly, clawing his hood into position.

The gunship landed and Paul looked back once, Annie, still protecting Natalia, huddled near the lashed-in-place German

146

Specials, a smile on her lips, her eyes sad.

And then Paul turned and jumped, after John Rourke, the snow so heavy now it was like a wash of tiny needles of ice against his face.

He hit the ground, not too hard, John almost lost already in the swirling whiteness of the downdraft. He was up, moving, following John Rourke as he had followed him for five centuries and knew he would follow him until the day he died. And a smile made his chill-numbed face feel alive for a moment. Heroes and sidekicks. John Rourke was the hero. Paul Rubenstein had once described himself as John's "faithful Jewish companion." Some things never changed . . .


Michael Rourke had elected to be first through the chimney, delegating Han Lu Chen to be last since Prokopiev, with his injuries, might be more prone to difficulty and, if he fell, he would need someone roped to him from above.

As he moved downward, Michael looked up, Maria Leuden scrambling after him, movement through the chimney an arhythmic combination of climbing, careful walking, occasional crawling, the chimney comparable to a narrowly winding stairwell, but irregular, treacherous and, as the rock surface made it appear, a freak of nature rather than a contrivance of man.

No map, no layout however rudimentary existed of the chimney, and as they moved ever deeper, there was no sense of where they were, how far they had come, how much of the journey remained.

As Michael looked back below him and moved on, he saw the chimney abruptly twisting right; there was no real concept of north or south here without consulting a compass and, with no idea of the composition of the rock, a compass might prove useless anyway.

The chimney seemed to twist into a low-ceilinged shelf and Michael reached the shelf, then reached up to aid Maria

147

Leuden in her descent, his hands going to her waist as he almost lifted her downward.

She was in his arms the next instant, and her arms encircled his neck. "I love you."

Michael kissed her quickly, then moved her aside farther along the shelf, helping Prokopiev down, too. "I do not wish to be kissed." The Russian smiled, laughing softly.

Michael shook his head and smiled, feeling his cheeks slightly flushed. "I hadn't been planning on it, Vassily—no offense." And the Russian clapped him on the back and limped off to join Maria Leuden, Han the next down. "Don't worry—I wasn't planning on it," Michael said cryptically, the Chinese intelligence agent just looking at him uncomprehendingly.

Michael Rourke took the German anglehead flashlight from where he had clipped it to the front of his parka, opening his parka as he used the light to explore the shelf on which they had stopped.

Maria was just ahead of him, whispering just loudly enough that he could hear her, "I think you should take a look at this, Michael." Michael Rourke moved more quickly now, beside her, and as he put his arm over her shoulders Maria Leuden whispered, "I am glad you only kissed me."

"Shut up," he told her good-naturedly, then drew her against him and kissed her hair. He pushed past her then, saying, "What was it you saw that you wanted—" But he stopped, just letting the sentence hang.

Directly ahead of him, through a niche in the wall, was a door, tight against water or air, it seemed, like a submarine door closed—and opened as well, it seemed—by means of a locking wheel. "Get Vassily and Han," Michael Rourke ordered, using the flashlight now as he dropped into a crouch beside the locking mechanism, examining it to determine age if he could.

It looked to be of familiar design, and the metal's integrity indicated it was either relatively new or exceptionally well made. There was tarnish in evidence, but it rubbed off to a dully gleaming brush finish under the pressure of his glove. Some sort of high-quality stainless steel with extreme surface hardness of perhaps a titanium alloy. The tarnish and the dust layer over it could have been the patina of centuries, or only decades.

Maria dropped to her knees beside him and he asked her, "What do you think? How old?"

But Han's voice from behind him offered the first attempt at an answer. "They could not fabricate such metal as this now. It is why they utilize the old weapons or copies of them. The Glock 17s of the pre-war Chinese Army, fortunately for the Second City military forces, at least, were among the most durable of pistols, it would appear." And as Michael looked over his shoulder toward Han, the Chinese hefted his own Glock, part of his standard Second City disguise but, Michael had noticed, something the intelligence agent seemed to carry otherwise as well. "The assault rifles were crude enough to be duplicated more crudely. But such as this door would be as impossible for them as the manufacture of a pistol like the one I hold in my hand. This door is from before the Dragon Wind, Michael."

"'Dragon Wind,'" Michael repeated. It was the Chinese term for the Great Conflagration, the fires which had consumed the sky and nearly consumed all life on earth. "Could this be—" He left the question unfinished.

"An access chamber into the missile silos," Vassily Prokopiev said, as if somehow snatching Michael's thoughts from the air.

"I think it could," Maria Leuden volunteered.

"It might well be fitted with an alarm," Han suggested.

"Five centuries old?" Michael asked.

"He is right," Maria said. "It wouldn't function anymore, would it, Michael?"

"Let's find out," Michael almost whispered, his fingers curling over the wheel and closing. He tried turning it, realized then that not only dust and tarnish had collected over the five centuries since its installation, but corrosion as well, despite the gleaming quality of the metal.

He gripped it more tightly, Prokopiev throwing his left hand to it, Han Lu Chen reaching across Michael's bending back, grabbing hold of it, Maria's comparatively tiny hands taking hold of the wheel as well. "Together!" Michael Rourke hissed.

And the wheel turned with a squeaking sound so loud that Michael thought it could wake the dead. And who knew what might be behind the door, for that matter?

# Chapter Twenty-Eight

The valley that spread before them and fronted the Second Chinese City could have been a biblical prophet's nightmare of Armageddon. Armageddon, perhaps, but not a nightmare, John Thomas Rourke knew. Because it was reality.

Had the lucky ones, indeed, been those who had died on the Night of the War? And if that had been World War Three rather than World War Last, then was he witnessing the beginnings of World War Four? Or, like World War Two in perspective against World War One, was it only a resumption of warfare merely briefly suspended?

He remembered history classes he had taken while completing the first four years of his university training. It was possible to trace World War Two's beginning all the way back to the Franco-Prussian War, the Japanese attack on Pearl Harbor back to Theodore Roosevelt's heavy-handed mediation of the settlement between the warring powers in the Russo-Japanese War.

History was an interlocking grid of wars, separated only by brief respites during which the antagonists might realign and re-arm.

Was the five centuries of the Sleep merely this?

"What are you thinking?" Paul Rubenstein asked him.

John Rourke looked away from the valley where Soviet ground forces and Second City Chinese forces battled to the death, where black Soviet gunships skimmed over the living and all living vanished in their wake, like angels of death. "That nothing has changed. It's time we were going." And John Rourke began moving back from the rocky overlook, the first few yards on knees and elbows until it was safe to stand and there was no risk of silhouetting himself against the gray sky. The threat of discovery from accidental aerial observation, however real, was a threat which could not be countered, only judiciously ignored.

They moved along the rim of the valley, ever nearer the mountain which was the heart of the Second Chinese City, where his son and the others had gone.

At any moment, if Maria Leuden's educated guessing proved correct, a missile might be launched, or the very mountain itself might explode as one or several nuclear warheads were detonated within it.

And, if the scientists were correct, the already fragile atmosphere, not yet recovered from the fires that nearly burned it away entirely five centuries before, would be dealt the death blow. Without planetary engineering techniques not within the technical grasp of a mankind for five centuries devoting all effort merely to survival, life on the surface of the earth would simply, irrevocably end, forever. The species Homo sapiens would have eradicated itself totally from the memory of the universe. Perhaps, if other life existed elsewhere, one of the robot probes of the Voyager type might someday be discovered and traced back to its planet of origin, a derelict rock devoid of all atmosphere and life.

John Rourke, the snow falling as heavily as before, his right gloved fist balled tightly to the pistol grip of his daughter's M-16, his best friend beside him, continued moving toward the mountain.

Time might, already, have run out.

# Chapter Twenty-Nine

Michael Rourke was the first through into the light, the light brilliantly white where it emanated from the base of the cylinder to which the air- and watertight door had opened, the cylinder itself extending downward seemingly without end. Here the light was gray, but by contrast to the pitch blackness through which they had moved, the blackness broken only by the beams of their flashlights, it was bright enough. Michael clicked off his German anglehead light and pouched it to his belt.

"Come ahead," he whispered, stepping down onto the rungs of a ladder which began here and extended downward toward the light. Above him, there was the solid face of the cylinder's top. As he had entered, he was initially fearful that the cylinder itself might be a missile launching tube. But capped as it was there, it could not have been.

Maria stepped out and he helped her onto the ladder rungs. He had tested them with his full body weight while still clinging to the door frame with both hands. It seemed completely sturdy.

"What is this?" Maria asked him.

"An access tube, maybe to the missile tubes. But the ladder points that way." The tube seemed almost polished and he wondered if it were closed at its base with another door similar to the one through which he and now Maria had just passed. But this door had identical-seeming opening hardware on the interior, identical except for an almost total lack of tarnish.

The air inside the tube had been stale-smelling, and when he had finally, with the help of the others, gotten the door open, there had been a popping sound, almost like the sound of a corked bottle of wine being opened in one of his father's videotaped movies at the Retreat.

Michael moved down along the ladder, Maria immediately above him, and Prokopiev passing through the porthole after her, Michael moving farther down along the ladder as Han Lu Chen, the last person, clambered through and onto the rungs just above Prokopiev. They were still roped together and Michael mentally opted for maintaining the arrangement. The rungs seemed sturdy enough but he intellectually refused to assume that the next one he stepped on would not give way. And he thought of his father's often heard words, "It pays to plan ahead."

Keeping his voice as low as he could and still be heard, Michael announced, "This is apparently an access tube. We'll follow it down until it plays out or branches off. If that Chinese agent got out this way, we should be able to get in. Han—close the door behind us and lock it."

"Yes," the Chinese intelligence agent answered, then set to swinging the hatch closed behind them. There was another popping sound, as though the gaskets surrounding it were self-sealing. Michael wondered fleetingly if the stagnant air supply would be enough to get them to their destination with the hatchway closed. But with it open, there was enhanced risk of detection should the shelf on which they had found the door be part of some regular guard route.

"Sound—even the sound of my voice—could travel a great distance in an environment such as this, so we have to keep sound to a minimum once we've started because we don't know what's below us. Ready?"

There were nods of assent. Michael started down.

# Chapter Thirty

Suddenly, there was motion all around her and there was gunfire and Sarah Rourke threw the muzzle of her STG-101 toward what she perceived as the enemy and prayed she was right as her finger touched the trigger, a loud burst and a bright, but small-diameter, flash, the gunfire making the self-compensating vision-intensification goggles she wore "blink," shutting down luminence as the brighter flashes came. It was like the old silent movies she had seen in museums and on television, the motion broken, distorted, jerky.

The STG-101 bucked in her hands, figures in line with its muzzle going down. And suddenly Wolfang Mann's voice was shouting in the bones of her inner ear from the radio set, telling her, "Move ahead quickly, Frau Rourke! I am with you!" And she heard as other orders were being shouted back and forth, the screaming of one of the commandoes as he died. The robot video probes were zig-zagging erratically as if suddenly they had lost all control and, when she looked back, it was the man who controlled them who was going down, dead, the monitor panels on the steady mount in front of him aflame, sparks crackling from them.

She ran, almost tripping over one of the robot video probes as it came toward her left ankle like some angry little dog.

A hand reached out for her and she thought for an instant it was Wolfgang Mann or one of the others, but in the other hand was a Soviet assault rifle. She fired first and the man's body rocked back out of the edge of her peripheral vision.

There was no way to keep count of the number of rounds fired, the cyclic rate so rapid.

She fired again as a figure fired at her, the tunnel floor in front of her ripping and shredding under the multiple impacts. The forty-round magazine was empty or the gun was jammed. In the semi-darkness and the confusion, with people all around her trying to kill her, there was no time to find out.

She worked the bolt for the under-barrel grenade launcher and actuated the self-contained triggering mechanism within the magazine itself, firing at a concentration of the Russian kill squad blocking the tunnel. The STG-101 bucked in her fists, there was a brilliant flash, and her ears rang with the concussion.

She found another magazine for the STG-101 and released the spent or partially spent one, letting it fall to the tunnel floor, ramming the fresh one up the magazine well, tugging at the charging handle, letting the bolt fly forward.

If the gun fired, it hadn't been a jam. It fired, another of the Russians going down, two more of them dodging clear of her.

Wolfgang Mann's voice. "Into the area past the explosion. Hurry! Then we use the grenade launchers! Hurry!" He wasn't talking just to her, she realized, running again, working the bolt for the grenade launcher, chambering a fresh round.

She fell, almost touching the grenade launcher's trigger, legs and arms splayed out on the tunnel floor, something dead inches from her face, human once, but the left side of the face blown away.

On her knees, her rifle still in her hands. Hands grabbed at her under the armpits and she screamed, trying to twist the muzzle of the rifle toward whoever it was— "Sarah! Hurry!" It was Mann beside her, almost lifting her straight up, half carrying her ahead as she ran beside him, his hands at her elbows.

They zig-zagged to avoid a body, jumped over another, Sarah nearly losing her footing in the sudden slickness that she knew had to be blood.

And they were past the point at which they were attacked, Mann shouting orders over the radio for using the grenade launchers. Sarah's was already ready to fire, and as the others formed around her and Colonel Mann and opened fire, she opened fire as well, her eyes squinted against the bright flashes as the grenades exploded. The tunnel seemed to shake with the successive multiple impacts, stray gunfire from the enemy force, then nothing but the crackle of flames as bodies burned.

She could smell the flesh and it sickened her, would have made her vomit, she knew, if she hadn't smelled the same thing before. "Reload," Mann ordered. She was already doing that, having exhausted the magazineload of grenades.

It was Schmidt speaking now. "The Russian prisoner died in the initial exchange, Herr Colonel."

"Poor bastard," Mann's voice cut in. "Other casualties?"

A short litany began, three dead including the remote video probe operator, and one wounded, but not so seriously he couldn't go on.

"We must find those Chinese troops. We are severely outnumbered here. Hurry on!" And he was propelling her forward. She kept her trigger finger outside the STG-101's guard, but kept the tumbler set to auto, ready . . .


"I am getting confusing radio reports," Otto Hammerschmidt called back along the fuselage. "There is so much radio traffic—wait."

Annie brushed a strand of hair back from Natalia's face, Natalia's eyelids blinking rapidly as though she were dreaming. The drug-induced sleep had seemed deep for a time, but now Natalia seemed more restless by the moment.

Hammerschmidt called back again. "The First City is partially under attack, the Soviet forces combined to the main entrance and to several key sections within the city, including the government complex. Our base that was going under

157

construction was overrun and Colonel Mann has taken personal charge. Those Communist assholes—excuse me—but they're in for trouble now, with the Herr Colonel running things!"

Natalia's eyelids still flickered, only more rapidly now. Dreaming . . .

His fingers touched the nape of her neck and found the hooks and eyes that closed the halter there and opened it, and as Natalia watched her own image in the full-length mirror, John Rourke behind her, the upper portion of her white dress fell away and her breasts were bare and she crossed her arms over her chest, covering herself with her hands, the nipples of her breasts hard-feeling and erect to her. His mouth came down on her neck and she shivered.

John—somehow the tuxedo he'd worn was gone—turned her around in his arms and he was naked. Her dress fell from where it clung at her hips, surrounding her ankles, obscuring her feet, and she realized that she, too, was naked. The hair of his chest felt wonderfully rough against her skin as she unfolded her arms, baring her breasts to him, and felt the first instant of contact between their bodies.

And Natalia started to cry as his lips touched her face . . .

Annie Rourke Rubenstein still studied Natalia's face, the eyelids moving more violently now, and, to Annie's amazement, tears flowing from Natalia's eyes and along her cheeks. Annie closed her eyes, somehow feeling like a voyeur.

# Chapter Thirty-One

John Rourke had planned ahead.

A ragged-looking group of Mongols, in a depression near the base of the mountain guarding a tunnel entrance Rourke was able to discern only because of the heat-sensing unit he had stripped out of one of the Specials, was slaughtering one of their own wounded. With the sensor, with which he had scanned the base of the mountain, he had been able to determine the location of the tunnel from several hundred yards away, then with Paul Rubenstein beside him had moved as close to the tunnel as possible for more detailed, visual observation. It was then that he had first seen the Mongols, known that the sensing device had revealed an actual entrance. Again with Paul beside him, he worked his way closer.

Now, seventy-five yards (approximately) from the Mongol position, John Rourke brought the M-16 to his shoulder, set to semi only, knowing Paul's rifle was set to auto and aimed toward the Mongol position as well, to back him up if he missed.

But John Rourke did not plan to miss.

Six men, discounting the seventh man on the ground who was being repeatedly stabbed with the Mongols' sabers, kicked by their fur-ruffed booted feet, spat upon—one of the Mongols even blew his nose on the injured man. Perhaps the man had demonstrated cowardice, perhaps some other undesirable trait, Rourke conjectured. But it was equally possible the

Mongols were just amusing themselves with someone who was dying anyway.

"Here we go," Rourke rasped, getting the farthest of the six men in his sights, then gently squeezing the trigger. With the first one, there was always more time.

The M-16 jumped slightly, the tinny sound of the action that was so noticeable when the weapon was fired semi-auto, and the farthest of the six standing Mongols fell.

As Rourke swung the Colt assault rifle's muzzle onto his next target, he considered the moral imperative that the already dying seventh man imposed: that he be helped. Rourke fired again, the second man's arms and hands flying outward, his saber sailing through the snow-filled air as his body slapped back into the rocks.

The third man was moving. Rourke fired. He stopped moving.

The fourth man was shouldering his assault rifle. "John— he's—"

"I know," Rourke almost whispered, firing again, the Mongol's rifle falling from his hands, his head twisting around, his body seeming to be dragged after it, falling.

The fifth man was running toward the tunnel the heat-sensing device had picked up. John Rourke tickled the trigger once again, the fifth man's body skidding off balance, forward, the man's hands grasping toward the small of his back as he fell.

The sixth man fired his assault rifle, spraying it into the rocks where John Rourke and Paul Rubenstein were, missing them by a good ten feet. John Rourke thumbed the selector to auto. "Help me out." As Rourke fired, Rubenstein fired, the sixth man's body racked with hits, twisting, lurching, slamming into the rocks behind him, his assault rifle still spraying, but skyward now, his right arm twisting with the torque, the gun finally falling as it fired out empty.

John Rourke was already moving, half diving into a snowbank, Paul coming after him.

Although the sounds of the battle between the Soviet attackers and Second City Chinese defenders were everywhere, the remote possibility existed that sounds of this brief battle might somehow be detected and bring more of the Chinese or, worse still, KGB Elite Corps commandoes.

As Rourke ran, he looked to right and left through the swirling snow, his eyes squinted against the huge flakes. No one was coming. He signaled to Paul to break left as he broke right, ramming a fresh magazine up the M-16's well, coming onto the concealed mouth of the tunnel in what some called a pincer formation, from the sides, closing on the objective. Rourke's right hand was numbing with the cold, but he hadn't trusted to a glove and there had been no time to replace it once removed.

They reached the Mongol position almost simultaneously, Rourke stepping over one of the dead bodies to aid the seventh man. But the eyes, wide open, staring upward, were already splotched with snowflakes.

Rourke exhaled over the eyes to melt the snow, then closed the lids. There had been no need to tell Paul to cover him; such was implicit. As Rourke looked up, then stood, Paul was methodically checking each of the other six. Rourke aided him.

"Mine are all dead."

"Mine, too," Rourke told him. Rourke looked behind them, toward the nearest location where there was a great concentration of troops from both sides fighting. But still, no one came.

Rourke safed his rifle and let it fall to his side on its sling, then found his glove.

"If I were starting a Glock pistol collection, I'd be in business. Same for the assault rifles. The sabers look terrible, almost as terrible as the rifles. No documents."

"I've got a Glock 17 at the Retreat. Fine pistol. Really durable, too. As I suppose the very existence of these proves. Leave the bodies—no time anyway," John Rourke concluded, walking quickly through the trampled-down snow toward the

161

concealed entrance his sensing device had shown was there, working his hand into the glove as he walked, opening and closing his hand to restore proper circulation.

Finding the entrance proved no challenge, a steel door—stainless, of reasonably good finishing qualities—was hidden half-heartedly at the rear of an out-of-place-looking stand of pines. Some boughs were broken where the tunnel had apparently been used recently. He examined a partially broken bough and from the liquidity of the pine sap, especially considering the cold weather, he judged within hours.

Rourke called to Paul. "Bring me one of those sabers—whichever one of them looks the stoutest." There was no reason to get his knife full of pine tar again. He turned, waiting for Paul to join him. As Paul ran up, Rourke took the saber from him, eyeballing it for an instant, then stepping slightly back from the stand and with a few downward cuts, hacking away a sufficient number of the pine boughs that they had clear access to the tunnel door beyond. He took the saber and tossed it javelin fashion into a snowbank a few feet away.

The door was, as expected, closed.

A ring handle was in place to the far left of the door, equidistant between top and bottom. John Rourke reached for it with his right hand as he heard Paul changing magazines in his M-16, Rourke's own rifle bunched tight in his left fist.

Rourke moved the door slowly open, inward. There was a terrible stench, strong-seeming even as the snowladen wind dissipated it.

Dull yellow light glowed faintly in the distance, between the meager light cast inward through the door, and the yellow light, nothing but blackness.

Rourke's right hand closed over the butt of one of the German anglehead flashlights. "Watch out." And Rourke depressed the switch, shining the light into the darkness of the tunnel. As quickly as he flicked it on, he flicked it off.

"What's the matter?" the younger man asked him. "What did you see in there?"

John Rourke flicked the light on again and he told Paul Rubenstein what he saw. "Human bones. Come on. Close the door behind you and mind you don't trip on a femur or something."

John Rourke stepped through the doorway, shining the light about him on all sides now. Oddly, he didn't instantly see a femur, but he saw human bones of all other descriptions. His left boot inadvertently rested on an anterior segment of a human skull. Human vertebrae crunched under his feet as he moved ahead.

"My God," Paul whispered.

"No—I think it has something to do with their god." Rourke moved into the darkness. And from deep within the darkness ahead through which they had to pass, he heard something that sounded like growling.

# Chapter Thirty-Two

Sarah Rourke's temples hurt from the sudden absence of the pressure associated with the vision-intensification goggles. But here, in the light of a vast recreation hall beyond a kitchen in which they had taken cover as one of the Soviet murder squads passed, there was light enough and wearing them was no longer required. She pocketed them in the BDU jacket, immediately setting to checking her rifle as the commandoes (only nine remained?) under Wolfgang Mann's command set to checking ways in and out.

As she satisfied herself as to the condition of her weapon, she suddenly realized she was terribly hungry. But there was nothing to eat, despite the fact she had just passed through a large, modern kitchen and that she was in a hall where, like as not, banquets were often held. All the weight of her rucksack was ammunition. A solitary canteen of water was on her belt. She didn't want to drink because, if she did, she might have to urinate and where could she do that? Sarah Rourke shook her head, disgusted. Where were the Chinese?

Wolfgang Mann's voice came to her through the radio and echoed her own thoughts. "Where are our Chinese friends?"

"I hope they brought Chinese food with them," Sarah told him. And then she shut off the radio. In the hall, they were close enough that they could speak to one another naturally. "I'm turning off my radio," she announced to anyone within earshot. Perhaps the radio chatter was giving her the headache.

There were two other sets of doors, besides the set through which they had entered, out of the kitchen, and a pair of Colonel Mann's commandoes flanked these doors now, preparatory to opening them, she assumed. One man from each team placed a suction-cup-like device, several inches in diameter, against the doors, the black rubber piece functioning like the bell to something analogous to a stethoscope, listening devices to detect what might lie beyond the doors.

There was considerable risk that the Chinese unit they were to have met had encountered one of the roving Soviet patrols, been killed or captured or even just delayed. Which would mean scrubbing the mission or penetrating the government center themselves without reinforcements and making the attempt to rescue the chairman of the First City on their own.

He was a decent man, the chairman, if somewhat naive, and deserved their best efforts.

She heard a snapping of fingers, started to speak aloud as she turned toward the sound, then, on impulse, hit the button to reactivate her radio. She nodded toward Wolfgang Mann, saying softly into the microphone, "I'm receiving."

"There is activity beyond the doors. This way," and he gestured for her to join him on the other side of the recreation hall.

She moved quickly, toward him, mildly surprised that she wasn't feeling greater fatigue as a result of the relatively sedentary lifestyle she'd been forced into by her pregnancy.

She stopped beside Mann and he raised a finger to his lips, signaling silence. Her eyes moved around the room. Colorful murals covered the upper portions of the walls, their theme apparently Chinese folklore, because there were dragons, princesses, scraggly-bearded men in flowing robes who looked like some cross between monk and wizard.

Mann's voice through her radio: "Schmidt—come in. Schmidt?"

There was no answer from the tall, very Nordic-looking Sergeant Schmidt whom Colonel Mann had left guarding the route over which they had come, by the doors leading from the kitchen to the corridors just fronting the end of the tunnel. "Schmidt?"

Still no answer.

Mann's face seamed with worry lines and he said, "Quickly—into the hallway. Standard entry pattern. On my mark!"

The remaining men of Wolfgang Mann's command moved out as if they were pre-programmed automatons, but she realized that it was training instead. One man on each side of the doorways, the others in an arc just behind them, weapons ready.

Mann joined the team on the left, Sarah stopping beside him until he pushed her behind him. "Close your coat. It has bullet-resistant properties, or did I mention that?" Awkwardly, with his left hand, he withdrew the antique Walther P-38 he carried, the STG-101 in his right hand only.

"No."

"Close it, then." And he turned his head toward the men at the other doors. "Be ready— Now!"

As her eyes moved to the doors nearest her, for the first time she realized the stethoscope-like listening devices had been removed and, where the doors seamed, there was a small rectangular object, black in color. She guessed an explosive charge and, in the next instant, both sets of doors blew open outward and in the well-lighted corridor beyond, she saw a dozen Soviet Elite Corps commandoes in their black BDUs, assault rifles at the ready, wheeling toward the explosions. But Mann's people fired first.

There was gunfire from behind them and Sarah automatically turned toward it, more of the Soviet commandoes pouring into the recreation hall through the kitchen doors.

She hit the bolt to cycle one of the grenades into the assault rifle's launcher, then pulled the trigger, the butt of the weapon braced against her hip.

As the first grenade exploded she was already launching a second, Mann beside her, spraying one of the forty-round magazines empty, the P-38 9mm firing from his left hand.

There were voices shouting commands, everyone speaking at once. Sarah Rourke kept firing the grenade launcher, unable to understand anyone clearly enough to know what was being said.

The Russians coming through the kitchen doors fell back.

Mann tapped her arm with the muzzle of his pistol, the slide locked back, the gun empty. "Sarah! Come with me!" And he was running, toward the blown-open doors. Sarah ran after him . . .

They had reached a landing and at the end of the landing, a long, high-ceilinged tunnel ran perpendicularly to the tube. It looked like a possible way into the Second City, perhaps through the missile-launching station itself.

The tube they had worked their way down seemed to go on forever.

Han Lu Chen carefully enunciated each word, as though his normally perfect English might be insufficient to the task of translating writing from his native language. The Chinese characters—each several inches high—covered approximately one hundred twenty degrees of arc of the tube's total diameter. "Any unauthorized access beyond this point will activate the defense system. Unauthorized persons should turn back immediately. Warning. Dangerous. Turn back."

"They're certainly explicit enough," Michael remarked.

Vassily Prokopiev volunteered. "Since I am less physically capable than any of you at the moment because of my earlier wounds, I am the logical person to go first."

"That's a great and noble thought, Vassily. But you're also less capable of running away from whatever gets started and we need you alive if we bump into any of your troops."

Prokopiev's broad shoulders shrugged under his torn Soviet uniform.

"I can—"

167

Michael looked at Maria Leuden. "No. Aside from the fact I won't let you, you've got the best chance of making enough sense out of their computer that we can enable an abort program." And Michael looked at Han. "And don't you start. I've gone first since we started down the chimney and there's no reason to change that now." Michael began loosening the knot holding the rope about his waist. "This may be bullshit," and Michael Rourke nodded toward the wall. "Or the defense system hasn't survived the centuries. Or maybe it still works. I'm going to put a lot more distance between us and we're changing the order, here. Han—you rope in behind me, but keep about twenty-five or thirty feet back. We've got rope to spare. Then Maria—you and Prokopiev rope onto Han. If they have electronic traps, they might have trap doors, anything. This way, if the floor goes out from under me, I'm covered but nobody's so close that if it's something else they'll be hurt. The important thing is that Maria's computer knowledge and Han's knowledge of Chinese come together at the fire-control center for the Chinese missiles. If they really are planning on detonating, that's the only chance we have to stop them."

Michael looked at Vassily Prokopiev and shot the KGB Elite Corps commander a smile. "And guess what that makes us, Vassily?"

"The word—it escapes me, but I understand."

Michael looked at him a moment longer. "The word's 'expendable.'"

# Chapter Thirty-Three

The growling in the tunnel darkness grew louder. "If we use guns, we'll attract whatever's human anywhere within a quarter of a mile at the inside, if the gunfire outside hasn't attracted them already."

"I understand, but I'm more worried about what isn't human," Paul Rubenstein whispered beside him.

John Rourke let the M-16 fall to his side on its sling. His right hand closed over the haft of the LS-X and he unsheathed it. He heard the snap closure on Paul's Gerber MK II fighting knife popping open, the sound of steel against fabric.

They began walking again.

From the darkness outside the cones of their flashlight beams, Rourke heard the sounds of footfalls and breathing so heavy it sounded labored. John Rourke wheeled toward the sounds, calling out to Paul, "Watch out from the left!" As Rourke swung the light, something out of a nightmare materialized less than a yard from him. It was a bear, he knew, on a rational plane, but the creature was horribly disfigured, one eye gone, the wound where the eye had been obviously from a burn. The bear's right front paw slapped toward him and Rourke dodged back, the bear coming at him again.

"Holy shit!" Paul Rubenstein half shouted.

"Watch out!" The bear turned awkwardly toward Paul Rubenstein, snarling at the flashlight in the younger man's hand, growling now as though somehow it were in pain.

John Rourke lunged, the LS-X held in his right fist as if it were a rapier, thrusting into the bear from behind against the area which in a human would have been the branches of the external carotid. But he felt the primary edge of his knife slip against muscle, the bear shrieking its anger and spinning toward him, Rourke backstepping just in time.

He aimed the light toward the animal's remaining eye, Paul visible in silhouette to its right side. Paul's knife stabbed downward, buried halfway to the hilt. The bear twisted, its face contorted in a rictus of agony, the right forepaw slapping backward, Paul Rubenstein catching its full force and thrown against the tunnel wall and down.

Rourke's right arm flashed forward again, the flashlight in his left hand still aimed toward the bear's solitary eye, the LS-X stabbing into the bear's throat. The hulking body twisted, Rourke still holding to the knife, wrenched from his feet, his fist still locked to the knife, the bear starting to fall on him. Rourke ripped at the knife, pulling it free, rolling right as the animal crashed downward, paws clawing at the tunnel floor, visible in the wildly gyrating beam of the anglehead which had fallen from Rourke's grasp.

Rourke threw himself onto the animal now, the LS-X in both fists, hammering down into the neck and head and shoulders, stabbing again and again, the animal's body heaving under him, the cries emanating from the creature at once frightening and pitiful.

The body seemed to convulse, and as the head turned right, Rourke drove the knife half the length of its foot-long blade into the side of the neck.

And suddenly all movement ceased.

Rourke let go of the knife and fell back from the animal to the tunnel floor.

"John? John!"

"I'm all right," Rourke answered the voice from the darkness. "How about you?"

"Knocked the wind outa me—holy—"

"Yeah." Rourke reached out for the anglehead flashlight, picked it up, shone the light toward the sound of Paul's voice, and already his friend was getting shakily to his feet. "Your light's over there," Rourke told him, seeing the second anglehead a few yards distant.

"I see it."

Rourke shone the light on the dead bear. There could be more creatures like this confined in the tunnel, but somehow he didn't think so. Paul's knife was still buried in it and, bracing his left foot against the dead animal, Rourke wrenched the blade free, then set it on the floor just out of the growing blood pool. His own knife had bitten deeper and was harder to extract, but he got it free.

"Should have tried grinning him to death like Davey Crockett did," Paul suggested, his voice still unsteady-sounding, no humor in it.

"Yeah, well, you try that technique next time and let me know how it turns out. And I'll loan you my knife just in case the bear's near-sighted." Bears usually were, one of the reasons why, in the wild at least, bears might attack when unprovoked, mistaking a human for another like itself.

"You bet," the younger man said, half laughing, but the laughter hollow-sounding.

With the flashlight, Rourke scanned the creature's body. Burn marks and other less immediately identifiable signs of mutilation were everywhere on the back and paws and head, clearly deliberate torture.

"Why'd they do that to him?"

"Bred him to be a maneater, then kept him set up with a constant supply," John Rourke almost whispered. "Deliberately caused him as much pain as possible, kept him enraged. He's the source of all our bones down here, or maybe he had a predecessor who contributed some of them. They're in various stages relative to approximate age—the bones."

"That's why they kept their zoo. To use the animals. Shit. The bastards—"

171

"It looks like that." Rourke nodded. "You up to moving on?" As Rourke spoke, he wiped the blades of both knives as clean as possible against the hide of the animal.

"Poor creature," Paul observed, his voice edged with genuine sadness. "What kind of people—damn them! This animal, the people they put in here for him to kill. What kind of people are they?"

"The kind of people we've come to stop from detonating a nuclear warhead. The bear was their watchman and executioner at the same time. Come on." Rourke sheathed his knife and started moving deeper into the tunnel.

At any moment, a warhead might be triggered and, Rourke realized, he would never know it because he would be instantly vaporized, just gone. Like shutting down a computer without saving the information fed into it, vanished.

The angle of the tunnel floor began to rise sharply, steadily, the light Rourke had seen from the doorway suddenly brighter now, yellow-looking still. They kept moving, no more strange breathing noises, no growls from the shadows. But what lay ahead, Rourke realized, might be far worse than a mutilated animal exploited to kill.

By the luminous black face of his Rolex—it was no longer dark enough for the luminosity to be effective and too dark to see the watch clearly, so he used his flashlight—almost an hour had passed since they had entered the tunnel, how much of that time consumed by the fight with the bear impossible to say. It could have been seconds, or several minutes, violence tending to dilate and distort one's perception of time, the more intense the violence the greater the perceptual distortion.

The bones were fewer here and considerably less concentrated than farther back and this caused John Rourke to consider that something near the end of the tunnel might have kept the bear away. What? Rourke wondered.

They kept moving.

"What do we try to do exactly once we get where we're going?" Paul Rubenstein asked him, his voice hushed.

"If they have a detonation program begun, we try to stop it," Rourke whispered back, stating the obvious. But he knew the intent of the younger man's question well enough. "If we can't stop it, then we try to think of something to neutralize or at least minimize the effect."

"You mean, if it's a missile, we keep it from launching and let it detonate inside the mountain. What about the other warheads, though?"

"That's a risk," Rourke answered after a moment. "A very real risk. But if it gets to that, there won't be that many options left anyway."

"What about Michael and the others?"

"There's a chance they'll get the job done and this will be unnecessary. But as long as there's a chance they won't— They've got about the same chance we have. Not very good." And Rourke felt a smile cross his lips as he clapped Paul on the shoulder. "But when's that ever stopped us, hmm?" Only idiots or persons with a death wish pursued hopeless danger— or persons with no other options remaining. Such had been the relationship between Rourke and Paul Rubenstein—no other options. Rourke thought back to the times between the Night of the War and the Great Conflagration. Then or now, he could have asked for no finer friend, known no braver, no finer man.

They kept moving, the tunnel floor rising so steeply now that it was like walking up a hillside, the added effort imposed by the incline slowing them.

But after another ten minutes as reckoned by Rourke's mental clock, the incline leveled suddenly, the yellow light now brilliantly bright and dead ahead of them.

Something inside John Rourke made his pulse race, his breathing faster. He knew the sensation well—fear. But he didn't know its cause. And that worried him more.

# Chapter Thirty-Four

Michael Rourke's eyes moved from side to side of the access tunnel, searching for some evidence of the electronic security measures warned against. Nothing. No out-of-place-looking seams in the floor, no photo-electric eyes, no speaker panels that shouldn't be where they were. The walls of the tunnel—well lighted, gleaming—were without feature, perfectly smooth and unbroken.

He stopped moving, carefully turned and looked behind him, Han there thirty feet back, Maria and Vassily Prokopiev behind Han. Nothing had changed.

And the tunnel seemed to go on forever.

For a moment, Michael Rourke wondered if he should turn back, return to the vertical cylinder which had led downward from the shelf off the natural rock chimney at the height of the mountain. But where would that route take them?

Maria called out. "Michael?"

And it started. His name, echoing over and over and louder and louder—"Michael? Michael? Michael? Michael? Michael? Michael? Michael? Michael? Michael?"

His ears rang with it, each time the word, his name, echoed, the sound louder, ever increasing in volume. His hands reached out to the wall surface and the wall surface vibrated in rhythm with Maria's echoing and re-echoing voice.

He looked back toward Maria Leuden. Her hands were to her ears, her mouth wide open. If she screamed— If he shouted to her not to scream— Han turned around toward her, the muzzle of his rifle clanging against the wall surface, the clanging repeating over and over and over and over again, ever louder, becoming part of the cacophony already surrounding them, Michael Rourke's ears throbbing with it.

Michael Rourke reached to his waist, slipped the hitch which bound the rope around him, throwing the rope down, running, Prokopiev's face contorting into a ghastly looking mask, not human-looking, the Russian officer falling to his knees. Han Lu Chen's fists beat against the wall, and the rumbling of his fists against the wall surface began to echo and re-echo and pulse along the length of the tunnel, the walls visibly vibrating now, like the tines of a struck tuning fork.

Maria was about to scream. Michael Rourke shoved past Han Lu Chen, half stumbled over the agonizing Prokopiev, threw himself on Maria Leuden, his left hand clamping over her mouth, his right hand smothering her face against his chest. Moisture dribbled down the sides of his neck and he realized his eardrums were probably bleeding, ruptured.

Blood poured from Maria's ears.

Han Lu Chen's body flopped against the wall, his knees buckling, his body collapsing. And Michael's eyes riveted to Vassily Prokopiev's right hand. A pistol, Prokopiev pointing it along the tunnel's length blood pouring from Prokopiev's ears and nose, his eyes wide. Mongols, with heavy ear protection, coming along the tunnel.

Michael risked the shout— "Nooooo!"

But the shout was lost in the already deafening roar. And then Prokopiev's body was clubbed to the floor of the passageway and Michael's insides shook and Maria's body wrenched against his as if she were in orgasm and the inside of Michael's head felt as if it were boiling over, the walls and floor and ceiling shaking, all hearing gone, his vision blurring, the pain beyond anything he had ever endured and the blackness sweet as a kiss.

# Chapter Thirty-Five

John Rourke stopped before the yellow light, separated from its source by a wall several inches thick and totally transparent, Plexiglas or something like it, the transparent material jointed every twelve feet by gleaming vertical metal strips, framed at top and bottom with identical strips, only shorter. The verticals rose hundreds of feet into the air. And beyond the wall lay an area the size of several football fields, its ceiling vaulted to the height of the mountain itself, it seemed. It was all here, under one roof. Unimaginably. Rank upon rank of auxiliary service bunkers connected by gleaming piping systems to more than a dozen breadloaf-shaped concrete structures. Piping into and out of demineralizers, turbines, condensate pumps, feedwater pumps, both main and auxiliary. Beyond these, running the length of the base of the mountain, disappearing over the internal horizon, transformers and storage tanks. And, visible in the mist-shrouded distance, tall, tapered-waist concrete smokestack-like structures. It was the largest fission reactor John Rourke had ever seen.

"This is how they run the mountain," Paul whispered, his voice sounding awed.

"This is why they've had power for five centuries. And it's a miracle they did. It has to be totally automated." There were panels of gauges stretching for hundreds of yards in either direction, untended, he knew, for centuries. No one here possessed the technological sophistication to read the panels. Of that he was certain.

Rourke began walking, his hand trailing along the Plexiglas, his eyes scanning the banks of consoles. After some minutes of walking in silence, he stopped. The Chinese of the Second City could not have comprehended what was here, judging from the barbarism they displayed. And John Rourke, for that matter, understood little of it. But no degree of sophistication was needed to understand the panel farthest rearward from them, at the center of the bank of abandoned instrument consoles before which they now stood, only the Plexiglas wall separating them from it. The panel was larger than all the rest and resembled a thermometer lying on its side. It held a large vertically running gauge and the indicator, for core temperature, was a third of the way into the red zone. "They're about to lose it all. It's melting down, Paul."

"Melting down—"

Rourke studied the machinery for several seconds, wishing Natalia were here with her superior knowledge of such things, her engineering and sabotage background an invaluable mix. "I just had a wild idea," Rourke almost whispered.

"What?" Paul Rubenstein asked, his voice flat, emotionless.

"If this is melting down, why isn't there an alarm sounding? And it would stretch coincidence beyond credibility that just when the Second City Chinese are about to detonate a warhead—if that is what they're planning—the reactor that's served them all these years just happens to go belly up."

"I don't understand what you mean. But shouldn't we get the hell out of here?"

"If it's leaking, we're already contaminated. So there's no sense running. Think about it. This was a survival retreat, like ours in Georgia, but on a much larger scale. The reactor was to keep it going—air scrubbers, electricity, water reprocessing, all of it. But between the Night of the War and what the Chinese call 'the Dragon Wind,' the Chinese here put their hands on a substantial portion of the People's Republic's nuclear warheads. Whoever was in charge here would only have done that for one reason—power. And not for light bulbs. But when the Dragon Wind came, it was realized that the core materials wouldn't last as long as they'd need them to last. Missiles were only useful for destruction, and destruction was already total. So—"

"You mean—"

"You're looking at the Chinese warheads, Paul. This—this—this huge reactor. The biggest I've ever seen, vastly bigger than anyone would ever need for any conventional use you could imagine. You could run fifty places this size, maybe a hundred off one-tenth the power this reactor could generate. And it's computerized, has to be. The computer is utilizing the nuclear material as needed, otherwise keeping the fissionable material rodded. And at the same time, it's a breeder reactor, producing more fissionable material than it uses. This entire mountain is a weapon and whoever built this was perfectly aware of that. No warheads, but one ultimate weapon. If this thing goes, the meltdown effect would be incalculable."

"I remember with the near misses before the Night of the War—" Paul Rubenstein began.

"The 'almost meltdowns.' They talked about the core material boring its way through the earth from one end to the other, didn't they?—and it sounded like something out of a bad science fiction movie, like the story they tell children that if you dig and dig and dig you'll dig a hole all the way to China. How about a Chinese boy digs a hole? And it's a mile wide and his shovel digs all by itself and very fast, so fast you can't stop it. And the other end of the hole is the Atlantic Ocean off the southern coast of Brazil."

"That'd—ahh—"

"Throw the earth's rotation off. Maybe rip the planet in half. I'm no physicist."

"How do we—"

John Rourke measured his words. "That steam at the far end by the cooling towers. It probably isn't radioactive. And we don't have anything to lose anyway. The control rods are pulling. Slowly would be the way for the maximum effect. Once they reach a certain height, the temperature will reach a certain level and it can't be stopped. It may have reached that already. If they started this as some religious ceremony, like Annie was saying Maria Leuden thought they might— If that was the way, then maybe whatever they did can be undone. They must have kicked a program into the computer and started all this. Maybe it can't be stopped by conventional means at all."

"Could we go inside?" Paul asked. "I mean, I know what'd happen to us. But—"

"There must be fifty rods in each reactor core. The control rods themselves could have begun to melt. Yeah. We could go inside. But I don't think we'd live long enough to get the job half done. Once we violate the seal on one of the containment buildings, the entire area will be flooded with radiation. Even with protective clothing, we wouldn't be able to hold out for more than a few hours. But we might have to go inside if that's the only way." And John Rourke looked at his friend. "Let's find their temple."

Rourke stepped away from the Plexiglas wall, feeling the odd pressure against the exposed skin between his glove and his sleeve, like a breath of wind where there shouldn't be wind at all, as his arm passed near one of the vertical joints for the enormous Plexiglas panels.

And suddenly he understood about the bear and why there were fewer bones the closer to the Plexiglas wall one came. He shouted, "Paul! Run for it!"

179

The wind was all around him now and electricity arced between his rifle and the right side of his body, and his body felt as if it were at once burned and stabbed and pain tore through him. Rourke stumbled, still trying to run, falling, blue and silver lines of electrical energy fluxing across the horizontals which supported the Plexiglas panels from below. Paul Rubenstein was shouting something incomprehensible, Rourke twisting his head around to see him, Paul's body twitching, the muzzle of his M-16 against one of the verticals, electricity arcing over Paul's chest, around his legs like bands.

Rourke fell flat, rolled onto his back, pain gripping his chest.

Electricity arced still between his rifle and the nearest of the verticals. Rourke's gloved right hand grasped his rifle by the plastic buttstock and he tore it sling and all from his body, flinging it against the wall of Plexiglas, the crackle of electricity louder now, the Plexiglas itself starting to blister.

He couldn't catch his breath.

His mouth wide open, gulping air, Rourke forced himself onto his stomach, his eyes feeling as though they would burst from his head, his eyes riveting on Paul Rubenstein. Paul was dying. Would die.

"No, damnit!"

Rourke lurched up to his knees, fell forward, Paul's screams subsiding, the electricity almost cocooning him now.

On his feet. The rounds in Rourke's M-16 began cooking off, bullets spraying in all directions as the controlless assault rifle bounced along the floor.

"Paul!"

A bullet gouged into the floor inches in front of Rourke's face, and the gun was silent.

The gun.

Rourke, his chest still knotted in pain, reached to his right hip, his right arm stiff, barely able to move. The 629.

He had it out of the Sparks flap holster.

Rourke stabbed the six-inch .44 Magnum Smith toward the vertical to which the flash deflector of Paul's assault rifle was melting. In a moment, Paul's rifle would cook off as well, he knew.

Rourke fired, Plexiglas by nature impact-resistant, the shot a miss, Rourke's right hand trembling so, his ears ringing with the concussion, the ricochet whining across the antechamber to the reactor compartment.

He fired again, hitting the vertical, ripping it half through.

An alarm sounded, the reactor compartment's integrity ruptured. Rourke fired again, then again and again and again, the ricochets only barely audible now over the howling of the alarm, the vertical metal strip severing, the electrical arcs across Paul's body dissipating for an instant. Rourke let the revolver spill from his fingers as he pushed himself up, hurtled his body against that of his friend, residual electrical charge ripping through Rourke's body, his left shoulder impacting Paul's right shoulder, his hands grasping Paul by the clothing, Rourke throwing his weight right and away from the severed vertical, both men tumbling to the floor, rolling.

All motion stopped.

Rourke lay gasping on the floor.

He forced himself up enough to see Paul. Paul wasn't breathing. Rourke threw himself over his friend's body, straightening Paul's upper body as best he could, raising the neck, letting the head loll back, forcing open the mouth. There was no time to check for obstructions. Paul didn't chew gum, didn't have dentures.

Rourke sucked in as much air as his own tortured body would allow, the heel of Rourke's left hand holding the forehead back, Rourke's first finger and thumb pinching the nostrils shut. He breathed the air into his friend's mouth, then again, quick, short breaths, four of them. Rourke released Paul's head, with the heels of both hands hammering down against the lower half of the sternum. "One . . . two . . . three . . . four . . ." His arms were so weary he could barely move them. ". . . thirteen . . . fourteen . . . fifteen!" He tilted Paul's head back, his hand under the neck again, reopening the airway, breathing into him again and again and again and again.

There was no pulse. "Paul!"

Rourke's hands hammered down against the lower portion of the sternum, then again and again and again and again.

"Paul!" Rourke shouted the name, his throat raw with it. "Paul!"

Again and again and again and again and again and—

A pulse. The eyelids fluttered. A cough. Another.

John Rourke collapsed to the floor beside his friend . . .



The roaring awakened him.

Michael Rourke opened his eyes.

He was cold.

There were faces looking down on him. Chinese faces. The lips moved and he could hear nothing except the sound which was always there.

He moved his head and spasms of pain fired through his head and his neck and his limbs. He was naked.

And one face stared down over his.

It was the woman who liked to see men die, the woman he'd met two days ago in the dungeon while the Russian sergeant was being slaughtered.

She was laughing at him . . .



Sarah Rourke listened as Wolfgang Mann spoke. It was all radio now, whispered so low that speech was barely audible. "The Chinese are not coming. We cannot get out of here. The Russians control more of the First City than we suspected originally. Only six of us, including Frau Rourke and myself, are fit to go on. Our only hope is to find the chairman and free him and then—to borrow an expression the Rourke family has used a time or two, one alien to us in the days of the Leader and the Nazism he preached—'pray.' Pray that the chairman can somehow marshal his people to repulse the invaders. Or otherwise, not only is the First City doomed, but so are we all. I cannot leave our injured unattended. I want two volunteers to stay with them. There is no cowardice in volunteering to stay behind. Perhaps it is the braver act than going forward. We, at least, will have mobility. Two volunteers and this God they speak of—may He go with you."

Mueller volunteered.

A young commando who looked barely old enough to shave volunteered as well.

Sarah Rourke looked at Wolfgang Mann's face, then at the faces of the two other men, Rheimenschneider and Franc.

"Divide up the ammunition evenly among us, one-third to those who stay behind, two-thirds to those who go on," Mann said quietly. "If we survive and are able, we shall return. And, if we are too late—your families will know. And"—Wolfgang Mann smiled a smile she had never seen on his face before—"if somehow you should survive and we do not, then to our families. Tell them that we tried and that no matter what happens, the freedom we have won after so long shall not be sacrificed." And then Wolfgang Mann did something which thoroughly frightened Sarah Rourke.

He went to Mueller and took out his cigarette case and handed it to the commando, and she heard him whisper something to Mueller about "Frau Mann" and she recognized the German word for love and Sarah Rourke's eyes welled up with tears . . .


Soviet gunships were everywhere now and Annie Rourke

Rubenstein wanted to scream, but Natalia Tiemerovna still slept, her eyelids still moving, the dreaming unending. Madness. Annie was crying and made no attempt to sniff back her tears.

Otto Hammerschmidt shouted, "I have fired my last missile, Annie."

In desperation, they had flown toward Lushun, fuel running low, the weapons systems nearly depleted, the First City surrounded by Soviet gunships.

In Annie's pocket was something given to her by her father. "If you are near the sea, and there are no other options, then open the cover and flip the toggle switch. And then pray a lot." And he had kissed her and hugged her harder than he had since she was a little girl.

It was before they had boarded the Specials to go out and search for Michael.

And now she understood what it was that he had given to her.

The liberated Soviet gunship Otto Hammerschmidt inexpertly but satisfactorily flew shuddered.

"We have been hit, Annie!"

She sniffed back her tears. More calmly than she thought her voice could sound, she called forward to him. "Otto— ditch in the sea. In the open sea."

"But—"

She had seen the place from which the signaling device came when all of them had gone there and been given the special medical examinations. But it was still like a dream.

Submarines.

An America of Americans of all colors and religions who fought the same war only against different enemies.

Annie looked at Natalia. Annie had already put Natalia into a life vest.

Perhaps it was all fate.

Fate that they should come here.

The engines which powered the main and tail rotors were

screaming like souls in torment, the very fabric of the machine creaked and twisted and shivered.

Smoke filled the fuselage. She coughed. Her eyes streamed tears.

Otto Hammerschmidt shouted, "We are going down!"

Annie Rubenstein felt a certain feeling of peace.

# Chapter Thirty-Six

The rifles were damaged beyond use. Paul Rubenstein's right hand and arm were burned and the fingers of his right hand did not close properly.

The muscles of John Rourke's chest and shoulders almost seemed to cry out to him each time he moved, cry out for him to rest.

They walked ahead, the Detonics Scoremaster .45s in Rourke's fists, Paul's left fist clenched on the pistol grip of the submachine gun he still called a Schmiesser.

Paul could call it whatever he wanted, John Rourke thought, smiling to himself.

Whether or not either or both of them had received a lethal dose of radiation, Rourke had no way of telling.

The alarm went on without end and, by now, John Rourke was barely aware of it.

There was only one purpose now.

The meltdown was under way.

It would be the last act of human folly.

John Rourke and Paul Rubenstein had spoken no words about it as they had crawled to their feet and started to walk. No words were necessary.

The one purpose was to find the temple, or wherever it was the religious zealots of the Second City had initiated the program, and to stop it.

If the program which began the meltdown was unstoppable,

no other purpose mattered.

All life would end.

"You're the best friend I ever had," Paul Rubenstein told John Rourke.

"Brothers," John Rourke told him.

"Yes. Brothers."

"Yes," Rourke whispered.

They walked on. Together.

# Chapter Thirty-Seven

There had been a design for a "safe" fission reactor, modular in construction and built for low output in the eighty-megawatt range, designed to be used in series with reactors of the same size, all geared to prevention of meltdown. Meltdown at the least would take the core material down through the earth beneath the reactor and into the underground water table. But some theories had held that a meltdown of sufficient size and heat would be unstoppable, punching through the earth from side to side.

If such were possible, a reactor complex of the size which powered the Second Chinese City would be capable of it.

They at last reached the end of the Plexiglas wall. There were metal stairs winding upward in a spiral toward a set of double doors, also of metal, these located some hundred or so feet above the floor.

"Just what I needed—steps," Paul Rubenstein said.

John Rourke looked at his friend for a moment, then said, "Stairs, actually. The general syntactual rule of thumb is that steps are on the outside of a structure and stairs on the inside."

"Just as hard to climb," Paul smiled thinly.

"Hmm." Rourke nodded, agreeing, then starting upward, the .45s barely grasped in his hands. Every muscle in his body ached and he imagined it was worse for Paul, falling in behind him.

The electricity began again, sparking along the metal

framework for the wall of Plexiglas, uncomfortably close considering what had happened, but of no danger to them now. Rourke imagined there was some sort of irregular time schedule, all part of the master program which ran the facility, this a defense system for the reactor complex. Perhaps some of the burns endured by the bear they had fought had been a result of being too close to the Plexiglas wall when the electrical charges were emitted, but the major disfigurement still was something Rourke put down to intentional mutilation.

A third of the way up the stairs, Paul called up to him, "Can we rest a minute?"

Rourke nodded, then sat on the stair nearest him. He had considered that the stairs might periodically electrify, but since they were the only way up and neither of them was in shape for a marathon, he had taken the calculated risk. The rubber treads, largely rotted away, had supported his theory that they were not.

"What do we do when we get there?"

Rourke looked down at the younger man. "Bluff our way through. Or maybe Maria can do something with the computer once we gain access to the program. If we can find Maria and if we can find the computer and if we can access the program. I don't know. The best we can?"

Paul Rubenstein looked up at him and smiled. "The best we can. Which, I suppose—"

"Right." And John Rourke, his back spasming with pain, stood, Paul grabbing to the railing and standing as well now. They started upward again, the electrical display winding down, the alarm still blaring but something Rourke was no longer more than passingly aware of.

At the height of the stairs, the doors seemed more massive close up than they had from the base and Rourke and Rubenstein stood before them, assessing them. "Could be electrified," Paul observed. "Once bitten, twice shy."

"Probably not an alarm unless this is some taboo area, and that wouldn't make sense because our Mongol friends outside had to have come this way since there doesn't appear to be any other way. Unless they came from the outside, and even then, somebody has to get down here with the sacrifices for the bear. And the hinges aren't lubricated but they aren't corroded as much as the rest of the metal, either. Which indicates they're opened and closed with some degree of frequency. They may be locked from the other side, however."

John Rourke tried the doors first by touching the muzzle of one of the Scoremasters against it to test for electrical shock, his hand only in contact with the rubber Pachmayr grips. No evidence of shock. "So far, so good," Rourke observed.

He rammed both pistols into his gunbelt and put his hands to the door handles. They twisted, the doors giving slightly toward him but not opening. "I bet they have a simple brace on the other side of the doors, just a crosspiece."

Rourke dropped to his knees, his muscles screaming in protest. He carefully inspected the seam where the doors met. There was a large rubber gasket on each door, but the gaskets were seriously frayed. On impulse, John Rourke drew the Crain knife from its sheath, gingerly inserting it between the doors, the gasket material falling away in chunks to the floor, some of the chunks powdering. With patience, he got the Crain knife's twelve-inch blade between the doors, well below the handles. He'd scratch the knife a bit, but it couldn't be helped. Slowly, he raised the knife until the saw-toothed spine of the blade encountered something solid. "I think I've got it." Rourke got up into a crouch, his back muscles locking up. He stood, waited a moment until the pain subsided a bit, then crouched again, this time more carefully. Steadily, he began to raise the knife, both fists molded to the handle, pushing upward, he hoped on the crosspiece.

There was a sudden increase of pressure, but only for an instant; then the pressure eased and there was a loud thudding sound heard from beyond the doors.

Rourke eased his knife from between the doors. It was a little scratched, but otherwise undamaged. He sheathed the knife,

Paul ready with the German MP-40 sub-machinegun in his left hand. John Rourke drew both doors open and stepped back, his hands snatching the two Scoremasters from his belt, thumbs jacking back the hammers.

A piece of wood about four by four in thickness and three feet or so in length lay on the floor.

The doors opened to a long corridor, the corridor well lighted and about midway along its length ornamental murals and lamps in evidence.

"The back door of the temple?" Rubenstein suggested.

"The back door of the temple," Rourke agreed.

Both men started into the corridor, not leaving the doors opened behind them, Rourke stopping to replace the wooden crosspiece. If someone were behind them, a proposition he doubted but refused to dismiss, he'd hear the crosspiece fall for some distance.

"Ready?" John Rourke asked.

Paul Rubenstein answered. "Yeah."

One of the Detonics Scoremaster .45s in each fist, the twin Detonics mini-guns under his jacket in the double Alessi shoulder rig, the 629 holstered at his right hip, John Rourke started ahead . . .


To be unable to hear was maddening.

Michael Rourke could see Maria Leuden, see her mouth opening and closing as she screamed, but he could not hear her. Han Lu Chen was shackled to the far wall, not bound to opposite sides of the massive altar as were Michael and Maria. And Han was being beaten across the back with a wide strap by the black-garbed executioner Michael had seen in the dungeons. On the floor between the altar and where Han Lu Chen was being whipped, the unconscious body of Vassily Prokopiev lay, discarded as though it were a child's doll no longer found amusing. The back of Prokopiev's head was blood-smeared.

Perhaps the sheer force of the sound had driven the Elite Corps commander to madness, or perhaps despair that all was lost when the chamber through which they passed had proven to be a deathtrap.

Strange feelings, Michael realized, but he respected the man and knew that under more normal circumstances, Vassily would never have fired a weapon in such a noise-expanding passageway.

The high priestess or whatever she was—very beautiful, very evil-looking too—was moving across the room. It was some sort of temple. With the long robes she wore, she seemed to float rather than walk. His eyes tracked her.

At the far wall of the temple, young women in white dresses paid obeisance to— It was a ballistic missile. Michael's stomach knotted.

Like a separate altar before the missile was the largest computer console Michael Rourke had ever seen in reality, like the controls for one of the old main-frame computers he'd seen in the occasional movie from his father's videotape collection at the Retreat.

And one of the women, very beautiful, would every few moments adjust the setting of a dial, depress a button, turn a toggle switch.

Maria had been right. They worshipped nuclear death here.

# Chapter Thirty-Eight

Paul Rubenstein shifted the battered Browning High Power from the tanker holster into the waistband of his pants, with the butt pointed left, the hammer down, ready for use with his left hand.

The Schmiesser was clenched tight in his left fist. He still could not move the fingers of his right hand without considerable difficulty and pain . . .

Michael Rourke could hear, but sound of any kind was like someone whispering at a seashore in the midst of a storm, almost more maddening than the total deafness which he had experienced until now.

He first realized he could hear again when, after a very long time, the woman who was the head of all of this, the priestess or whatever, came to him and raised her fingernails over his face, like cats he had seen in videotapes, claws distended, about to claw him, he thought.

And he heard Maria Leuden, who had stopped screaming (he'd seen her mouth stop opening and closing, seen the tendons of her neck cease to distend, seen the flush in her cheeks dissipate), either passing out or drifted off to sleep. Suddenly she screamed again—but this time Michael Rourke really heard her.

The black-robed torturer with the strap with which he

continuously beat the seemingly unconscious Han Lu Chen, turned toward Maria and shouted something doubly unintelligible because of Michael's hearing and the fact that the torturer spoke Chinese, a language with which Michael had almost no familiarity.

The woman turned away and Michael Rourke saw Vassily Prokopiev, who he had thought was dead, Prokopiev's face smeared with blood. Prokopiev staggered to his feet and snapped his left elbow up into the face of one of the Mongol guards (there were at least a dozen and a half of them). Prokopiev grabbed the guard's Glock 17 pistol and shot the guard twice in the face, then shot the priestess or whoever she was in the back.

The woman fell to the floor.

Prokopiev had one of the Mongol swords and, as he collapsed, blood spurting from a facial wound, he hacked downward with the sword and the rope beneath the blade severed and Michael Rourke's left hand was free . . .


John Thomas Rourke positioned both Detonics Scoremasters in his pistol belt, the .45s cocked and locked.

He had heard shots.

At the end of the long corridor, murals on the walls depicting the Night of the War and the Great Conflagration and other scenes unrecognizable other than in their violent themes, two large doors stood, ornately carved, black-lacquered wooden doors with trim that appeared to be real gold.

John Rourke tried the doors and they opened, despite their apparent considerable weight, opened easily under his hands . . .


Michael Rourke's right hand grasped the Glock 17 pistol as it fell from Prokopiev's other hand, Michael's fingers stiff, moving with difficulty. But he was able to make the pistol fire a

194

pair of 9mm bullets into the face of the nearest of the Mongols, who was charging toward him with his saber drawn.

Michael twisted right, the span of rope between his right wrist and the steel ring to which the rope was tied less than three inches. Michael fired, the whine of the ricochet making him want to retch, it was so close. But the rope was severed.

He sat up, his head swimming, stabbing the pistol toward his bare legs, firing once to free the right ankle, two shots before he hit the rope binding his left ankle.

A third Mongol was coming and, as the saber crashed toward him, Michael Rourke tumbled from the altar, hitting the floor hard, the stone cold to his nakedness . . .


Paul Rubenstein twisted his body weight left, throwing his already injured right arm against the doors, figuring he had nothing to lose.

As the doors burst inward, John Rourke stepped through.

Both Scoremaster .45s came to John Rourke's like living things coming because they were called.

And both spoke.

Paul Rubenstein, the pain in his right arm like a thousand toothaches, rammed the Schmiesser forward, taut against its sling, firing.

Mongol guards were going down.

Women in long white dresses who looked as if they were late for some sort of prom rushed across the room—it was a temple—and brandished torches. It was shoot at the women or burn, but he fired into the temple ceiling. Some of them fell back.

John laced one of the women across the jaw with his fist, a pistol still clenched in it as he dodged a torch.

Maria Leuden was lashed to some sort of pagan altar, naked, screaming. One of the prom girls came toward her in a dead run, stabbing a torch toward her face. "John!" Paul swung the Schmiesser on line with the torch bearer's chest.

195

But there was the crack of a pistol shot, then another and another.

Paul's eyes shifted left. Michael, stark naked, one of the Chinese Glock 17 pistols in his left hand.

As Michael just stood there for an instant, two Mongols charged him, guns and sabers drawn.

"Paul! Get them!"

The boom of John Rourke's .45s, emptying as Paul stabbed the Schmiesser in the men's direction and sprayed.

Paul saw it coming and dodged, a saber slash, but his footing went and he sprawled back. Paul fired out the Schmiesser, the Mongol going down.

Doors on the far side of the temple were opening, more Mongols streaming through.

John Rourke's .45s were still. Rourke rammed both pistols, the slides still locked open, empty, into his pistol belt, drew the 629 and fired from the hip like some sort of western gunfighter, one of the Mongols down, then another and another, the temple walls echoing and re-echoing with the concussions.

Michael Rourke passed like a blur across Paul's field of vision as Paul found the butt of the Browning, thumbed back the hammer and shot another of the Mongols twice in the throat.

As one of the Mongols charged John Rourke, John fired, the Mongol's body jackknifing but, incredibly, not falling, carried forward by momentum. John Rourke raked the barrel of his revolver across the man's forehead as he came, the Mongol going down.

A man all in black, a wide strap half like a whip, half like a belt of enormous proportions, rushed forward, the belt lashing out, John's left shoulder taking the impact as John tried to turn. Paul Rubenstein fired as he clambered to his feet, then fired again and again and again, the black-robed man stumbling to his knees, the whip falling from flaccid fingers, the body tumbling forward.

John Rourke's revolver emptied into another of the Mongols, then Rourke sidestepped, twisted awkwardly right, his left leg rising, his left foot double-kicking another Mongol in the groin and abdomen as the man charged.

John Rourke dropped the revolver into its holster, both hands moving, the twin Detonics mini-.45s coming from under his coat.

One of the temple maidens in the white prom dresses hacked toward John's face with a torch, John stepping back and firing the little .45 in his left hand, the torch splitting in two, sparks showering the woman, her dress catching fire.

She ran, screaming.

Paul Rubenstein threw himself toward her, onto her, smothering the flames with his body, the woman reaching up to claw at his eyes. "Sorry—" Rubenstein backhanded her across the jaw with his left fist which still held the pistol.

John Rourke was moving through the crowd of Mongol mercenaries like someone wading through a pool, the little Detonics .45s barking once, then again, then again, men falling on either side of him.

Paul was on his feet, firing the Browning High Power. At the far left edge of his peripheral vision, he saw Michael Rourke, Michael looking at once ludicrous and deadly. Michael was naked except for his double shoulder holster. The Berettas Michael carried were in his fists and firing, men falling as Michael fought his way toward his father, killing at point-blank.

Rubenstein emptied the High Power, dropped to his knees as he rammed the pistol into his belt, then grabbed up one of the Glocks still holstered on the belt of one of the Mongol mercenaries.

Paul Rubenstein got to his feet, the Glock tight in his left fist. He fired, fired again and again, fighting his way now toward John and Michael.

Maria Leuden shrieked, "Help me!"

197

Paul wheeled toward her where she was still bound at the opposite end of the altar. As he turned, he saw Michael turning, John moving, a blur. A Mongol with a torch rushed down on her. Paul fired and, as he fired, heard almost simultaneous shots from beside him, the Mongol's body jerking, jerking, twisting again, flowers of blood at the Mongol's forehead, his throat and his right cheek.

Paul turned quickly back toward the doors through which the additional Mongol mercenaries had come.

No movement, except for a few of the Chinese women in their prom-like dresses who ran toward the corridor beyond.

"Paul! Help me close those doors!" Michael streaked toward the door and, despite it all, Paul Rubenstein almost laughed, because streaking was exactly what it was, Michael Rourke still naked.

John called, "I'm freeing Maria—my God! Han! Paul. Michael. You get Maria."

Paul looked back as he threw his weight to the door, Michael against the other door. The doors were twelve feet high at least, but easily enough moved. But, as Paul closed his door of the pair, his eyes swept across the room and found John Rourke. John was freeing Han Lu Chen of chains which bound him to the black marble wall nearest to the altar, Han's body striped by the whip, almost unrecognizable as human.

The doors slammed to with a clang, Paul's eyes shifting from the beaten Han Lu Chen toward the walls on either side of the doors, searching for a brace with which to keep them closed.

"Paul! Here!"

Michael Rourke was tugging at a mighty bar, resting along the joint between floor and wall on the far side from where Paul stood. It looked to be at least eight by eight inches and as many feet in length.

Paul ran to him, bent to the bar, tried lifting it.

Without warning, John Rourke was beside them, at the center of the bar. "Ready! Lift!" The bar was up and they guided it toward the doors, raising it still higher to drop it into the cleats on the door.

It fell into place and the doors trembled.

"Han's in desperate shape," John Rourke rasped. "But we're in worse shape if we don't stop that meltdown."

Michael was shouting and Paul couldn't understand why until he noticed the bloodstains beneath Michael's left ear and, as Michael turned his head, a similar blood trail under his right ear and along his neck and onto his chest. "What meltdown?"

"A series of nuclear reactors—" Paul began, but realized Michael couldn't hear him. "Reactors! A bunch of them! Could screw up everything! Boom!" And Paul gestured outward with both hands and his right arm seized with pain.

"Right." Michael nodded.

Vassily Prokopiev was on the floor, seriously wounded as well, it appeared, and Michael dropped to his knees beside him. "Paul? Cut Maria loose?"

Paul finished reloading the Schmiesser, started to speak, only nodded, drawing the Gerber and going toward the altar to cut Maria loose. He couldn't help but notice—and didn't think Annie would really mind—but Maria Leuden had a very pretty body. Between Maria and, earlier, helping to dress Natalia, he was seeing a lot. But there was only one woman he wanted to see and, by now, Annie would be safe somewhere with Otto Hammerschmidt and Natalia, too . . .


Annie Rubenstein clung to the life raft, but the raft was going down, one of the Soviet gunships passing over them moments earlier, strafing the raft, wounding Otto Hammerschmidt, then flying away, leaving them to die in the water.

The raft, partially deflated already, could barely hold Otto and Natalia well enough to keep their unconscious forms sufficiently above water to be able to breathe.

Annie had gone into the water to reduce the downward pressure on the leaking raft.

The signaling device her father had given to her—Annie had

activated it the moment the stolen Soviet gunship Otto piloted had almost shattered against the calm surface of the Yellow Sea.

No one was coming.

"We need you! Damnit! Help us!"

No one was coming.

# Chapter Thirty-Nine

Sarah Rourke had found a place to go to the bathroom and she felt better now.

"Sorry," she said, rejoining Wolfgang Mann and the other two men.

"For what are you sorry, Sarah?"

"I mean, holding you guys up."

Colonel Mann smiled that very nice, very sincere smile of his and told her, "Each of us is a unique person. Your persona happens to be female and biological needs cannot be ignored. You have nothing to feel sorry about. If I had at my disposal one hundred commandoes with your courage and skill, no enemy of freedom would ever stand before me and survive."

"You're very nice." It sounded lame to her as she said it, but it was the only thing she could think of to say.

Mann smiled again, saying nothing.

With the two remaining commandoes, they set out again, the terrain familiar to her here, the lower levels of the government building where, presumably, the chairman of the First City was being held prisoner. She hoped he still lived, prayed that he did, because the chairman was now their only hope. There had been three sentries near the entrance she had selected—a service access—and using silenced pistols the sentries were dispatched almost too easily.

It was then, after entering through the service access, she had found a bathroom and used it. Something was making her stomach very queasy and she kept telling herself it was the baby.

They walked along the corridor toward the service elevators now.

The feeling of unease grew in her. They passed a storage room.

She heard a sound that she couldn't identify, from the elevator bank.

"Inside here—it's a feeling—"

Mann rasped to his men, "Follow Frau Rourke! Hurry!"

She passed through the doorless doorway quickly, flattening herself against a stack of crates just inside the opening, Mann and the others just behind her. She could hear their breathing through the radio. She hissed, "Shh," once and held her breath.

The sound of elevator doors opening.

Then the sounds of Russian voices.

Boot heels clicking against cement.

Through the opening, she could see men moving, black Battle Dress Utilities, Soviet assault rifles.

In their midst was a man dressed in the uniform of an Elite Corps colonel.

For one split second she caught his face in profile.

It had to be.

Sarah Rourke loosed her rifle and drew the Trapper Scorpion .45, as she stepped from hiding whispering, "Back me up, but only when I say to." She felt Mann's hand reach for her, but she slipped out of his grasp.

Sarah Rourke dodged between two KGB Elite corpsmen carrying assault rifles slung at patroling positions, then punched the muzzle of her .45 against the face of the man in the colonel's uniform, praying it was Antonovitch, the new commander, with Karamatsov dead. "Freeze!" She didn't know the word for it in Russian but shrieked the word in English as loudly as she could, thumbing back the Trapper Scorpion's hammer to full stand as she said it, the hammer going back making a loud click.

Rifle muzzles were pointed at her from all sides. If Mann would only trust her as much as he said he did, trust her that way now.

Her left hand was knotted into the back collar of the colonel's uniform blouse.

For an instant, no one moved.

"Tell 'em I'm a Rourke and I'll kill you, so help me God!"

The colonel spoke, first in English. "What can you hope to gain, Mrs. Rourke?" But sweat was beading on his forehead.

"Tell them!" She pushed the muzzle harder against his cheek, drawing the pistol back then just a little because she remembered something John had told her, that a Colt-Browning pattern .45 wouldn't fire with firm backward pressure against the muzzle because it pushed the slide out of battery.

It had to be Antonovitch. She prayed it was Antonovitch.

He spoke in Russian.

There was a blur of movement from the entryway to the storage room, Colonel Mann and his two commandoes stepping out, assault rifles going up, getting the drop on the dozen or so KGB Elite corpsmen.

"What do you—" Antonovitch began in English to her.

"Shut the hell up. You do exactly as I say or this gun goes off and even a dumb Commie like you knows what a .45 will do at this range. Colonel Mann!"

"Yes, Frau General?"

She almost started to laugh. "Disarm these guys and if anybody gives you any lip, Antonovitch here gets it." And said to Antonovitch, "Tell your people. Tell them!"

Antonovitch spoke to them and she relied on Mann's knowledge of Russian—which was very little—to recognize whether or not Antonovitch was playing it straight.

Quickly then, Colonel Mann and his two commandoes began stripping the Russians of their weapons, tossing rifles, pistols, individual explosives, knives, all into the storage room.

"Now," she told Antonovitch, "out of their uniforms, down to their underwear. Men don't fight so well without their pants."

Antonovitch smiled a little thinly. And, she gave him credit, he had guts. "What if they aren't wearing underwear, Mrs. Rourke?"

"I worked as a nurse, I've got a husband a fully grown son and I'm pregnant. You've seen one, you've seen 'em all. Tell them to strip! Now!"

Again, Antonovitch spoke, the looks on the faces of his men telling her that he'd said exactly what she'd told him to say.

Quickly, but with obvious reluctance, the Elite corpsmen began to undress. She was almost surprised they didn't wear black underwear.

Colonel Mann, who was obviously enjoying himself, ordered his men to throw the uniforms into the storage room as well.

"No—get one of them to help you. All the guns and other stuff into the elevator. That's where we're going."

"There are troops up there—" Antonovitch began, panic filling his eyes, his voice shaking a little.

"Good. And the chairman?"

He didn't answer her. Mann was having the clothing and weapons moved.

"And the chairman?" Sarah Rourke repeated, punching the .45 against his face again.

"Yes."

"Good." My God, she thought, she had to urinate again . . .


Maria Leuden sat at the computer console. "I can't read Chinese. It won't do me any good." There was nothing in John Rourke's musette bag that would revive Han Lu Chen. But— "Michael!" John Rourke called across the temple floor to where Michael Rourke was tending to Prokopiev's wounds with materials from Rourke's musette bag. The Russian was sitting up, very weak-looking but as likely to live as any of them. "Michael? Did you bring a first aid kit from one of the Specials?"

"Yes. There are enough—"

"Bring it over to where Paul's tending to Han."

Rourke left Maria Leuden—she was half dressed but decent—and ran across the temple toward where Paul was using the German antiseptic healing spray on Han Lu Chen's back. John Rourke dropped to his knees beside the man, his own back spasming with pain.

As Michael joined them, Rourke took the first aid kit Michael carried and searched for the pre-prepared syringe of synthetic adrenaline.

He could kill Han Lu Chen by injecting it directly into the heart, but if he didn't risk the Chinese agent's life, then the whole world might die.

"Turn him over and hold him down. If I don't do this right, he's dead and so are we," John Rourke almost whispered to Paul and Michael.

He prepared the syringe.

# Chapter Forty

If only Michael were here, Annie thought, almost verbalized. He was such a strong swimmer. But it was miles to shore. She told herself she shouldn't have told Otto Hammerschmidt to ditch in the water. She should have taken their chances with the Russians over land.

"Help us!"

She screamed the words, swallowing water and almost starting to choke.

The raft was so deflated now that, by treading water, she was barely able to hold up Natalia's and Otto's heads, keeping them out of the water.

She had stripped away her heavy clothes and was only in her blouse and her underwear.

Her pistols and Natalia's were suspended on their pistol belts over a still floating piece of wreckage a few yards distant. The little Cold Steel Mini-Tanto was still strapped to her ankle.

What if sharks came? The little knife—that was all.

"Help!"

The signaling device was in the pocket of her blouse, over her left breast. It probably didn't even work anymore after the prolonged exposure to salt water.

Her father had told her about the sharks when they had traveled to Mid-Wake for the medical examinations, and she had even seen one (at least she thought it was one) through the video monitors at the front of the submarine.

But none of the friends he'd made were there except the cute little nurse who had told her that her father was so stubborn, and of course, Mid-Wake's president. Handsome and such a wonderful voice. But none of the others had been there, all off in their submarines fighting the Russians or whatever they did.

And suddenly, Annie Rourke Rubenstein was seized with panic. What if the signal had worked and, instead of summoning help from Mid-Wake, it had summoned the Russians they fought beneath the sea?

She looked around, the surface of the sea churning slightly, definitely less calm than it had been. What if—

The raft was all but totally deflated and she supported the weight of Natalia and Otto almost completely, her arms weary with it. What would she do when she could no longer support them both? How would she choose who was to die?

She was crying.

"Help!"

But no help came . . .


Sarah Rourke kept the .45 against Colonel Antonovitch's temple as the elevator doors opened on the upper level of the government building where the chairman's apartment was, where the rooms she and John used and all of them used were located.

In a strange way, it was like returning home.

"You will never escape here alive," Antonovitch said with surprising calm as she pushed him out of the elevator and into the corridor.

"What happens to us, happens to you," she advised, wondering how long she could keep this up.

KGB Elite corpsmen began running toward them along the main corridor.

"This is where you decide to live or die," Sarah Rourke whispered to Antonovitch. His eyes flickered toward her. "Tell them to lay down their arms and use the elevator, then send it back for the next batch of your guys." His men were closing rapidly, Colonel Mann and the two German commandoes armed with their own weapons and Soviet weapons taken from the men they had disarmed, ready to open fire. "You'll die first. I swear it!"

Antonovitch shouted something in Russian and the Elite corpsmen slowed, stopped, waited, their rifles at high port, ready to swing on line and fire. "After everybody's out of this building," Sarah Rourke said hastily, "and Chinese troops have retaken this section of the city after your men evacuate here and all the rest of the city, then withdraw beyond the mountains. You have my word as a Rourke that you'll be freed, unharmed, allowed to rejoin your men outside the city. We'll even give you free transportation." She just realized she had never disarmed Antonovitch of his pistol. But it was too late to try that now.

"The German—he will listen to you?"

She shouted to Colonel Mann. "I told him—"

"I heard what you told him, Sarah." And Wolfgang Mann looked directly at Antonovitch. "I will honor Frau Rourke's pledge, Herr Colonel. You have my word as a German officer."

Antonovitch started to say something, apparently thought better of it.

"Bring out the chairman. And if somebody puts a gun to his head, you die," Sarah told Antonovitch.

"This time, it appears that you win. It is too bad that history has dictated that the Rourke family should be the intractable enemies of the Soviet people. Otherwise, but—"

"History didn't dictate anything," Sarah Rourke told him, the pistol still at his head. "Men like Karamatsov and you, just ordinary thieves and killers until you put on uniforms and tell yourselves you're heroes and what you're doing is for the good of some crazy historic destiny—men like you made the choice. And this time, you'll live. Next time you won't. Bring out the chairman."

Antonovitch barked orders and an officer from among the

corridor guards put down his rifle, issued more orders, and the men around him, slowly at first, put down their weapons. The officer and two other men disappeared along the corridor and, for a moment, she forgot she had to urinate because she thought that maybe Antonovitch had some trick up his sleeve.

The seconds seemed to wear on forever.

One of Colonel Mann's commandoes began offloading the Soviet weapons from the elevator, then began gathering up the weapons the guards had put on the floor.

Her head ached. Her hand felt stiff holding the pistol so rigidly. Her knees were locking because Antonovitch was taller than she was and she had to stand as tall as she could to keep the gun at his head properly.

And then, his robes mud-splattered, hair uncombed, the chairman of the First City was brought into the corridor. He glanced once to either side of him and the Soviet guards left him. With his customary dignity, he walked alone down the corridor, past the Russian troops who had held him prisoner.

He stopped before Sarah Rourke, bowed slightly and smiled. "How good of you to come, Mrs. Rourke."

Sarah Rourke wanted to laugh and cry at once—and she still had to go to the bathroom—but she held the pistol to Antonovitch's head while his men started filling the elevators.

# Chapter Forty-One

Han Lu Chen, Michael and Paul holding him up, leaned forward in the chair before the console. "That button on the keyboard. Try that button." His voice was so weak that it was barely audible.

Maria Leuden pushed it and the monitor screen flickered, a mixture of Chinese symbols and English words appearing. Immediately, Maria began accessing the program.

Vassily Prokopiev's voice came from behind them. "I apologize for killing the woman. It is likely she knew the program you seek to invade."

"Likely," John Rourke said without turning his head to look back. "Prokopiev?" And now Rourke did look back.

"Yes, Doctor Rourke?"

"I notice that this computer seems to be set up for guidance systems monitoring."

Prokopiev, head bandaged heavily but face alert-seeming, leaned against the wall beside the doors, a brace of Glock pistols on the floor beside him. In the last several minutes, there had been the sounds of concerted hammering on the doors. Mao's guards, Rourke imagined, trying to retake the temple. At mention of monitoring the missile while in flight, Prokopiev sat up straighter.

"Would you and Paul," Rourke began again, "be able to convert the monitoring system so you could contact your forces outside the city? Alert them to pull back in the event we can't stop this—although, in honesty, that wouldn't do much good for them, just buy them a few moments, perhaps. But—"

And he followed Prokopiev's eyes as they moved upward along the length of the missile. "I could call down a gunship to land near the opening through which the missile would launch."

"You could, yes. But I don't exactly relish the idea of getting killed by the KGB any more than dying here."

Prokopiev smiled. "Certain death is always the poorer option."

"Get Paul to help you. He's good with electronics. Then go call your friends. And I'm going to need Paul as soon as you have it set up." And John Rourke looked at Paul Rubenstein.

There was an odd look in Paul's eyes.

Maria Leuden spoke. "I accessed a monitoring program. The missile will launch in eighteen minutes. I don't think I can stop it."

"What about the meltdown?" Rourke asked her. He sat beside her, as calmly as he could, fresh loading the magazines for his pistols.

"I do not know yet," she answered, her voice low.

"Try that line—with the character that looks like a tree," Han advised.

Maria began working the keyboard again . . .


Annie Rourke sank below the surface, realizing instantly that she had passed out or fallen asleep, and as she forced her head above the water, she gagged, her eyes scanning the water for sign of Natalia or Otto. She held to the deflated life raft. She started under the surface again, though, coughing as she gulped air.

Otto Hammerschmidt. She saw him, reached out to him, dragged his head toward the surface. She coughed water as she screamed, "Natalia! Natalia!"

And the water suddenly began to foam and hands reached

out for her, figures in black clothing and helmets. She almost lost her hold on Otto Hammerschmidt as she reached for her little knife, but a hand like a vise caught her wrist.

The helmet of one of the figures surrounding her. It was pulled off. The head ducked below the surface and reappeared all wet, curly hair matted over the forehead. "I'm Jason Darkwood. And you must be Annie Rubenstein, the five-hundred-year-old man's daughter. Anybody else in the water?" He had a handsome face, even all wet.

She realized she was dead and this wasn't happening. Annie Rourke Rubenstein said, "Natalia," anyway.

The man who called himself Darkwood nodded and began talking again, but not to her. "Sebastian? How's Major Tiemerovna? We got her?"

Nothing for a moment, then, "Good. Prepare the *Reagan* to surface. Mark on our transponders. Put out a raft for us. In just another second here, repeat that last part to this charming young lady I've just found. I suspect she'll be an interested listener."

And the man with the flippant attitude and the pretty eyes passed over something to her that looked like an ordinary earplug, putting it beside her jawbone. And she heard a voice in her ear, deep, resonant, cultured. "I have been instructed by Commander Darkwood to inform you that Major Tiemerovna has been brought in by two of our divers who immediately administered a hemo sponge so she would be able to breathe. We have every reason to suspect that Lt. Commander Barrow will be able to bring through Major Tiemerovna most satisfactorily. Thank you."

She was holding the little thing against her jawbone and she dropped it, Darkwood fishing it out of the water, then pushing his hair back from his forehead. "You're the one my father talked about!"

"The smart ass—that's me, I'm afraid." And Darkwood smiled at her, then held the little plug against his jawbone and spoke. "Lieutenant Stanhope—talk to me."

And he put his head beside hers with the earplug-like thing between them and she could hear, too. "Captain—this man's been seriously wounded, but I think he'll make it. Over."

Darkwood looked at her.

"Hammerschmidt," she said. "Captain Otto Hammerschmidt. He's a German commando. He's my friend."

"I know the name," Darkwood told her. And then he spoke through the little earplug thing again. "Tom—that man's an officer with the forces of New Germany. Make sure he makes it. Darkwood out."

She almost screamed as a massive black monolithic shape began to rise out of the water about twenty-five yards from them.

"That's my submarine, the U.S.S. *Reagan*. You'll love it. Trust me."

Somehow, she did.

# Chapter Forty-Two

In case what they planned worked, with Michael helping,
John Rourke had dragged the bodies of those Maidens of the
Sun (as Han had called them) who had been left behind down
the corridor and beyond the steel doors leading to the staircase,
just above the reactor room. Bound with parts of their own
clothing, but loosely enough that once they regained
consciousness they could eventually work themselves free, at
least there they would have a chance to survive the back-blast
of the missile firing.

Prokopiev, with Paul's help, had contacted the Soviet force
outside the Second City, established his identity and ordered
up a chopper with a volunteer crew, then ordered the rest of
the Soviet force to the mountains well away from the Second
City.

John Rourke wished Natalia were there. But, by combining
Paul's and Michael's and Prokopiev's skills with his own, the
barely conscious Han Lu Chen assisting Maria Leuden as best
he could while she worked the keyboard for the main portion of
the computer, there was, at least, a chance.

Prokopiev and Michael, Prokopiev with considerable
difficulty, had climbed the gantry and were, John Rourke
hoped, having some success with the onboard guidance
system. It should be a matter of gyroscopic adjustment only,
Rourke hoped. To attempt to sabotage the entire guidance

system might only have the opposite effect and precipitate premature firing.

John Rourke knelt beside Paul at the rear of the massive computer, Paul rewiring the interior of a large gray panel, the covering off. "What I hope I can do and what Maria says might work," Paul began, "and what would be a hell of a lot easier if my right hand weren't so stiff, is to set this sucker up so we can keypunch new guidance coordinates into the system. Maria said it and she's right. There isn't any time to get into the memory tapes and fool with them. I saw systems like this, hybrids. Transitional types of computers, half keypunch and half not. We can fool with the keypunch, like Maria's doing now, but we've gotta make it talk to the other part of the system. Get a handshake, like they used to say."

Six minutes remained before launch, six minutes before the meltdown of the reactors would be beyond recall.

It was a doomsday machine, crude, but of the highest order of lethality.

The missile was programmed to launch and return to point of origin upon re-entry, the radioactive core material of the myriad reactors already punching through into the earth as the missile struck. The largest explosive device ever conceived. And the most deadly.

"How much time, John?"

"Just under six minutes."

"Shit—"

Rourke stood up, walked quickly to where Maria Leuden was working the keypunch. "How's it going?"

"I think I've got the new coordinates set. But if we only figured them right." They had punched up a master program of guidance coordinates and improvised. All that remained was to feed the new coordinates into the system.

"So—all I have to do is put the card under that sliding pressure plate—"

"And push this button—I think," Maria told him.

215

"You start up the gantry."

"What about Han?"

Rourke looked at the Chinese, half unconscious now, head resting on the work surface before the master console. "I'll take care of Han. Promise."

He took her by the elbow and walked toward the gantry. "Paul? Almost?"

"Almost—maybe."

They stopped at the base of the gantry. John Rourke looked upward, shouting toward Michael. "How's it going?"

"We have realigned the gyroscopic and inertial navigational controls—we think," Vassily Prokopiev called down.

"Then get up by the hatch so you can get out as soon as the final firing sequence begins and the hatch opens. Maria's on the way."

"What about you?" Michael shouted down.

"Don't worry," Rourke said uselessly. He helped Maria to the gantry ladder, stayed there as she started up, then returned to Paul.

Paul didn't look at him as he spoke. "This thing's either going to work, or cook off all the wiring in the system and fire the missile without altering the trajectory. So." With some difficulty, Paul stood up. "How much time?"

John Rourke glanced at his Rolex. "Three and one-half minutes."

"Now what?"

John Rourke reached out his right hand.

Despite the injuries to his right arm, Rourke knew, Paul did the same.

They clasped hands.

"I mean—if this is it, hadda be a real handshake," Paul said quietly.

"Help me with Han."

"I'm staying."

"What about Annie?" John Rourke asked quietly.

216

"She'd stay, too. You'll never make it up without me with Han on your back. Who you kidding?" Paul grinned.

John Rourke nodded and their hands parted.

Rourke moved quickly toward the keypunch console, picked up the card. He placed it under the pressure plate in the card hopper. "She said to push this button," John Rourke said.

"Then I guess we'd better push it." Paul smiled.

John Rourke felt the corners of his mouth rise in a smile. "Then I guess we'd better push it."

John Rourke pushed the button.

Nothing happened. But what was supposed to happen? It was a gamble. And life was the only game he'd ever gambled in.

"Help me with Han."

Paul slung his sub-machinegun behind his back, then helped John Rourke to get the injured Chinese into a standing position, Rourke bending forward, letting Han Lu Chen collapse over his left shoulder.

Rourke stood there a moment, settling the man's weight as best he could. Then he looked at Paul. "Let's go."

Together, they started for the gantry.

"You first in case you need a push with that extra weight, huh?" Paul suggested.

Rourke nodded, put his left foot to the first rung, then started to climb.

The missile, mere feet from them, began to vibrate noticeably. They kept climbing. Rourke glanced at his watch as he moved his left hand toward the next higher rung. Less than two minutes.

Exhaust smoke began to exit from the base of the missile.

A low, rumbling sound began.

One minute even, now.

The missile began to shake, the gantry ladder shaking too now.

Forty-five seconds.

The hatch was open above them, the gray sky visible, Michael looking down through the hatch opening. John Rourke wanted to shout up to him to get away. But Michael would not have gone.

Climbing.

Thirty seconds.

The very fabric of the mountain seemed to shake.

If the reprogramming worked, the meltdown procedure was aborted, the trajectory of the missile changed.

If. Fifteen seconds. The missile started to lurch upward.

Retaining cables on all sides of the missile snapped away.

John Rourke reached upward toward the hatch. Han's weight—

Michael's hands reached down.

John Rourke could feel Paul pushing upward on Han's body.

Michael grasped Han by the hands and raised him upward, and then there were other hands, black uniform blouses, KGB Elite corps commandoes.

Rourke climbed through the hatch, reaching back, with Prokopiev pulling Paul through. A Soviet gunship was ready to lift off just a few yards from the open hatch in the top of the mountain.

One of the Elite corpsmen reached for John Rourke's guns. John Rourke's hands moved. Prokopiev shouted in Russian. "No time. To the gunship!"

Claxons sounded.

The mountain shook.

Great clouds of noxious-smelling vapors issued from the hatchway, Rourke and Rubenstein and Prokopiev running for the chopper on the heels of the Elite corpsmen. "Lift off!" Prokopiev was ordering.

The gunship started to rise, John Rourke at its base, Paul clambering aboard, Rourke and Prokopiev boarding together.

The gunship slipped left across the mountaintop and started to climb.

John Rourke crouched beside Maria Leuden. Han Lu Chen's head was in her lap. Michael's arm was around her shoulders.

The missile.

Out of the hatchway it came, hesitating against the gray sky, then rising, so enormous that it seemed impossible, like some optical illusion.

But rising.

"Did you do it?" Prokopiev asked beside Rourke.

Paul answered. "If we aren't vaporized in—"

"Three and a half minutes," John Rourke supplied, looking at his watch. "Or, if the center of the mountain doesn't seem to collapse. If neither one happens, we did it."

The gunship, per Prokopiev's orders, hung back about a mile distant from the mountain of the Second Chinese City.

Wind and cold whipped at them, but John Rourke didn't think any of them cared.

John Rourke's eyes flickered between the mountain, visible through the open door in the fuselage, and the mountain.

If it worked, the meltdown would be halted and the process reversed.

If it worked, the missile's trajectory had been altered enough so it would not re-enter, but arc back miles above the atmospheric shield and go off harmlessly into space.

If.

The face of his Rolex.

The mountain.

No gray-white streak passed between them an instant before blindingly brilliant light and oblivion.

And the center of the mountain did not collapse.

John Rourke stood up. He slid the fuselage door closed.

"Now what?" Rourke asked Prokopiev.

"I shall drop you wherever you wish within reason and then face a court martial." Prokopiev smiled, extending his right hand.

John Rourke took Prokopiev's offered hand.

219

His thoughts were filled with concern for Natalia, that her mind would be restored, with concerns for his family, that someday they would find peace. And, as he clasped Prokopiev's hand, this Russian who might be shot for his humanity despite his position as head of the Elite Corps, John Rourke also considered the concepts of hope and honor.

# JERRY AHERN

## SURVIVALIST 16: THE ARSENAL

Marshal Vladimir Karamatsov was dead. With his arch-enemy gone, John Rourke, CIA-trained weapons and survival expert, should have been able to sleep secure in his bed. Certainly the assassination squad that burst into his room must have hoped they would catch him off guard.

But as he shot it out, he could not know that a terrifying new threat was looming up out of the East. Not just a personal threat, but the threat of another nuclear holocaust being unleashed on an already war-ravaged world by a sadistic madman.

As John Rourke stalked the last would-be assassin down the night-time corridors, his Trapper Scorpion .45 cocked, his work was only just beginning . . .

A Royal Mail service in association with the Book Marketing Council & The Booksellers Association.

Post-A-Book is a Post Office trademark.

## JERRY AHERN

## SURVIVALIST 15: OVERLORD

For John Rourke, CIA-trained weapons and survival expert, it looked like a rendezvous with certain death.

His arch-enemy Vladimir Karamatsov, armed with a devastating gas that can transmute normal men — and women — into homicidal, blood-crazed animals, is about to seize control of a huge nuclear arsenal.

Like few men alive, John Rourke knows the full horror of thermonuclear war. Although the odds against survival, let alone success, have never been longer, he knows he has no choice but to attack and destroy this terrible threat.

**HODDER AND STOUGHTON PAPERBACKS**

# JERRY AHERN

## MID-WAKE

John Rourke, CIA-trained weapons and survival expert, was fighting for his life – underwater!

There had been other survivors of the nuclear nightmare that had devastated the world generations before. Far beneath the ocean's surface, a hidden war was raging between Russians operating from their huge, multi-domed sea-bed city and the Americans of Mid-Wake: their secret sub-Pacific military complex.

But now the Russians, realising that earth's surface was habitable, had begun to emerge. Only John Rourke, escaping from his captors, armed with a pair of the enemy's Sty-20 dart-firing sedative guns, could warn his allies that an evil underwater empire was about to rise out of the waters . . .

**HODDER AND STOUGHTON PAPERBACKS**

## THE SURVIVALIST SERIES